Lord Havergal took Lettie's arm and escorted her back to the curricle. "It is not necessary to apologize, Lettie. You would not be in alt to meet a vicar or curate, and you are not impressed to be dining with a viscount—and a poor wasted viscount with his pockets to let besides."

"Quite so, especially when said viscount is only here with a view to conning me into padding out those pockets."

"Conning? That is a hard word, ma'am. It suggests deceit. Begging is more like it."

"Come now, Havergal. Admit you want the blunt to pay off your gambling debts."

"Will it change your mind?"

"Certainly. My opinion of you would be better if you at least told the truth."

"But would you forward me the money?"

"No."

THE NOTORIOUS LORD HAVERGAL

Joan Smith

FAWCETT CREST • NEW YORK

A Fawcett Crest Book
Published by Ballantine Books
Copyright © 1991 by Joan Smith

Library of Congress Catalog Card Number: 91-91835

ISBN 0-449-21846-5

Manufactured in the United States of America

First Edition: July 1991

Chapter One

Lᴇᴛᴛɪᴇ ʙᴇᴅᴅᴏᴇs ᴀɴᴅ her companion, Miss Fitz-
Simmons, were just finishing breakfast when the
butler entered the morning parlor with the post.
Lettie's main interest in this daily event was always to see whether there was a note from Tom,
her younger brother, who was on the edge of graduating from Oxford. Her sharp eyes espied a
franked letter in the bunch, and she gave a *tsk* of
annoyance. Her acquaintance with peers and members of Parliament was slight. The only gentleman
of her acquaintance possessing the privilege of a
frank was Lord Havergal, and he was the last person she wanted to hear from.

Miss FitzSimmons flipped through the post and,
finding nothing for herself, examined her friend's
letters instead. "There is a letter from Tom. And
another letter for you, *Mr.* Beddoes," she said
archly, handing them over. Violet FitzSimmons was
a widgeon, but not even she was dense enough to
mistake her friend for a gentleman. It was her mo-
notonous little joke; she repeated it every time Lord
Havergal wrote to his testamentary guardian, Miss
Letitia Beddoes. Havergal innocently assumed

L. Beddoes to be a gentleman and addressed his letters to her accordingly.

Lettie put Havergal's pesky letter aside and opened Tom's first, to see what new items he required to cut a dash at Oxford. Tom's toilette was impeccable, but his letters were invariably stained with tea, wine, jam, or at the very least, inkblots. This time it looked like jam.

Violet FitzSimmons waited impatiently to hear what Tom had to say. "Waistcoats," Lettie read, scanning the short letter. "His have become so stained, they are beyond cleaning, and his pockets are to let. I can let him have a few guineas of my allowance. We do not want him to make a poor impression at university. He will be graduating soon and must be in fashion when he goes up to London to seek a position."

"Tom would look well in stripes," Violet said, her eyes assuming a faraway look as she envisaged her favorite in an elegant striped waistcoat. "Narrow stripes have a slimming effect," she explained. "Not to say that Tom is chubby. He has practically lost his baby fat."

"Well he might! He is one and twenty now and master of all he surveys, so long as he does not survey beyond the five hundred acres of Laurel Hall."

It occurred to Miss Beddoes that Violet ought to try the slimming effect of stripes herself. At five and thirty, she was filling out to matronly proportions. The extra pounds suited her face well enough. Her cheeks were full and youthful, her brown eyes were still bright, and her hair was hardly touched by frost. But when she stood, her spreading figure whispered, "middle age."

There was no danger of Miss Beddoes letting herself go in this indulgent manner. With the estate to take charge of since Tom left, her body was more muscular than when she was in her teens. Mr. Norton, the only gentleman who took any sort of proprietary interest in her, frequently told her she was "too lean." But then his favorite animals were pigs, so she did not harken to his opinion. Yet she had noticed recently that strangers, upon first meeting Violet and herself, took them to be of more or less the same age.

As she was eight years younger, this did not entirely please her. Her mirror told her she had lost the first flush of girlhood, but she was by no means raddled. She blamed the error on her authoritarian manner. As resident mistress of Laurel Hall since her papa's death a year ago, everything was left up to her. An equivocal manner and hesitant commands ask to be disobeyed. She learned that much the first month and altered her style accordingly.

Lettie possessed an air of dignified maturity. Her black curls were pulled back severely, revealing a chiseled nose and firm jaw. A broad brow, gray eyes, and pleasant smile completed her visage. Her gowns, always of the best materials if not the latest cut, were held to be unexceptionable in the narrow society of Ashford. Mr. Norton told her the haughty way she held her head lent her an air of distinction, and Violet told her she was sick and tired of hearing her praised for her "countenance," when what she *was* was bossy. Miss Beddoes paid very little heed to either of them.

"What has Lord Havergal to say, Lettie?" Violet inquired, before giving her a minute to read the letter.

She slit it open and perused it, murmuring the gist of it as she read. "His shooting box . . . Cotswolds . . . wants to protect this valuable property . . . new paint . . . possibility of adding ten acres . . . A thousand pounds," she said, closing the letter with the inevitable sense of discomfort that always accompanied these requests.

"Lord Havergal spends a great deal of money, does he not?" Violet said, shaking her head. "I mean to say, this twenty-five thousand his cousin Horace left him was spoken of by the family as a mere drop in the bucket where Havergal is concerned, yet he seems to be *constantly* pestering you to get hold of it."

"Viscount Havergal will inherit a great deal of money when his father dies, but Lord Cauleigh enjoys excellent health. Meanwhile, Havergal has a more than adequate allowance, along with a few inheritances from other relatives, like that left him by Sir Horace."

"I don't quite understand how it is that Sir Horace Wembley is both Havergal's cousin and yours, yet the two of you are not related and have never even met," Violet frowned.

"Sir Horace was Havergal's cousin; he was married to some cousin of my mama's. The Beddoes were connected to him, not related."

It was a connection the Beddoes cherished, as it was as close as they came to touching nobility. The family was genteel, of course. They lived in some provincial splendor at Laurel Hall, in Kent. Mr. Beddoes had been an astute gentleman and had always contrived to keep several thousand pounds ahead of the grocer. Sir Horace, when he was alive, had been accustomed to discussing his investments with Mr. Beddoes. They became the best of bosom bows, and when Sir Horace died, he made Mr. Beddoes the executor of his estate. Lettie's farseeing father realized he was no younger than Sir Horace, though of somewhat better health, and suggested a coexecutor be named in case he died before the trust was terminated.

"There is no one who understands the ins and outs of your affairs so well as my own Lettie," Papa said. "It is a pity she were not a gentleman, and we could make her coexecutor."

"Why, it is not illegal for an adult lady to act in such matters, is it?" Sir Horace asked, stroking his chin. "I seem to recall my own mama was guardian of some nieces. . . ."

"Well, but Lettie is only three months older than your heir. This Havergal would not care for having a young lady holding his purse strings."

"Oh, as to that, the dab I am able to leave won't mean a thing to Havergal. Lettie will only have to see that the Consols are paying their five percent and send the interest along to Havergal each quarter. I would leave it to him direct, but the lad runs through money like water. It will be well for him to have a little nest egg set aside. Whatever you do, don't let the lad get his hands on it, or it will be gone within a fortnight. I will arrange that he assume the capital on his thirtieth birthday. I trust Havergal will be married and settled down by that time, and you will still be alive and kicking till then, eh Beddoes?"

Within three months of Sir Horace's demise, Mr. Beddoes was carried off by a heart seizure. Lettie had just turned twenty-six when she became testamentary guardian to Lord Havergal in the matter of Sir Horace Wembley's endowment. She was now twenty-seven, and for the past year, she had let Havergal live under the misapprehension that she was not only a gentleman, but a gentleman of advanced years. His letters invariably inquired about her gout. Where this gout came from, she could not imagine, except that her papa used to complain of it, and Havergal perhaps assumed it to be a family failing. He seemed to think Lettie was her father's brother.

She had written him a kindly letter at the time of her father's death, outlining the legal situation and assuring him that she was willing to do what was in her power to assist him. Unaccustomed to business communication, she had signed it L. A. (for Anne) Beddoes and received a very polite reply addressed to Mr. L. A. Beddoes. She did not correct the error, as she felt he would take directions more kindly from a man.

The next letter from Havergal was equally polite. It suggested that in lieu of quarterly payments, it would be more convenient for him to receive all the interest on the estate in a lump sum at the first quarter. L. A. Beddoes replied promptly: Was Lord Havergal aware that this would mean an entire year with no income, as it would take twelve months for one year's interest to accrue? The next missive from Lord Havergal was less polite. L. A. Beddoes had misunderstood his intentions. Would he please continue with the present arrangement till further notice. During the ensuing months, Havergal had tried by a number of transparent ruses to get his money out of her. He had suggested various schemes that were bound to make him a fortune, but L. A. Beddoes squashed them all.

It was inevitable that Violet and Miss Beddoes should take an interest in this quasi-ward, and as Violet was an avid reader of the social columns, they were not long in the dark as to just what they were dealing with. It was a rare journal that did not have some account of Lord H's doings, and a rarer one that had anything good to say of him. He was a fixture at the balls, races, plays, operas, and other amusements that the *ton* offered. Lord H was mostly famous for being extremely eligible, but there were also mentions of his nags, his gambling, his toilette (the Havergal cravat evoked a few cartoons), his women, and his pranks.

It was Lord H who took a blanket and pillow into the House of Lords and was ejected when he began snoring. This was in protest against the government's refusing to debate his bill on the redistribution of rotten boroughs. A staunch Whig, he reproached a fellow Whig by painting the door of his house, on Half Moon Street, Tory blue when that gentleman wrote an article in favor of increasing Prinney's income. "One would have thought he could commiserate with *that* request," Violet said with unusual acuity. They were well aware by that time that Havergal had a prodigal way with money.

Through all that interesting year, they had only the vaguest idea of Lord Havergal's appearance, based solely on poorly drawn cartoons in the journals. Some showed his jaw unusually large and square. Another gave him a curl in the middle of his forehead and lashes an inch long. All cartoons agreed in outfitting him in the first style of elegance, with broad shoulders and intricate cravats. And all suggested in different ways that they were parodying a handsome gentleman.

"I wonder what he really wants the money for," Lettie mused. "Could it have anything to do with the new fad of pig racing in Green Park we were reading of? I seem to recall Lord H's name occurred. Hand me the latest journal, Violet."

Violet reached to the table behind her, and they began rifling through the pages. "Here it is," she said, handing Lettie a page.

Lettie read aloud, " 'PIG RACE IN GREEN PARK DRAWS CROWD. The handsome Lord H's entry, Hamlet, was judged the fastest trotter. Unfortunately the porker could not decide in which direction to run. Like his namesake, he vacillated at the critical moment and lost the race. Rumor has it that Hamlet's poor sense of direction cost Lord H a thousand pounds.' " Lettie set the paper down. "That sum sounds familiar, does it not? It is not Havergal's shooting box in the Cotswolds that requires a

7

thousand pounds, but his creditors. I shall deny his request—as usual."

Violet spooned sugar into a fresh cup of coffee and said, "I wonder where they find jockeys small enough to ride pigs. Do you suppose they use children? It would be dangerous."

Lettie kept her lips steady and said, "I shouldn't think they use jockeys at all, Violet."

"Ah, that would explain the pig's running the wrong way."

"It does not explain how a grown man can waste his time on such folly. I'll answer Tom's note and Havergal's letter, and then we'll drive into Ashford. I mean to have a new shawl for the spring assembly. The fringe of mine has knotted so badly, I cannot get it to hang free, even with my comb."

"Mr. Norton will like that," Violet said coyly.

"Oh, as to Mr. Norton, it is you who ought to be buying a new shawl. I'm sure it is you he comes to see."

This joke was nearly as fatigued as Violet's calling her friend "Mr. Beddoes." For five years Mr. Norton had been dangling after Lettie, and for five years Lettie had been trying unsuccessfully to divert his interest to Miss FitzSimmons. Violet, she suspected, would not dislike the diversion.

There was a time within living memory when Mr. Norton had been only a yeoman farmer, but when some relative died and left him the largest hop farm in the neighborhood, he suddenly became a gentleman. He remained true to his first love—pigs—and true also to his second—Letitia. It was not his low origins that displeased her in his role as suitor. It was his age: four and forty was a trifle long in the tooth for her.

As well as the two large properties, he also had a good character, a jolly temperament, and the staying power of Job. He kept coming back after every rebuff, smiling, joking, and showering her with hams, suckling pigs, and tales of the barnyard, till she didn't know whether to laugh or scream.

The drive of three miles into Ashford was beautiful in late April. The fruit trees were just coming into bloom. They looked like large balls of cotton, swaying gently in the breeze. The hops, a feature of the countryside, were in bloom, too, hanging in yellow clusters from their training poles. The pointed cowls of oasthouses for drying the hops were another distinctive feature of the landscape.

Mr. Norton had removed from his more modest pig farm to Norton Knoll, the hop farm, when he became a gentleman. The ladies passed it en route. The house, one of the oldest in the area, was built of stone brought from France by the Normans and erected in the Norman style. It was in all the tour books. Yet its impressive size and interesting architectural features failed to enchant Lettie. Mr. Norton must inevitably accompany the house. Not even Norton Knoll was worth that sacrifice.

It was Violet whose head skewed to the right to search the estate for a sign of him as the carriage sped past. She apparently didn't spot him, for she didn't say anything.

"How much are you going to send Tom for the waistcoats?" she asked when they were beyond the boundaries of Mr. Norton's land, and any hope of seeing him had diminished.

"Three guineas. That should buy him two waistcoats."

"I shall send him one as well, for sugarplums. Tom does love his sugarplums."

"Tom is no longer a boy, Violet. He'll probably buy wine with it. The scholars are allowed to keep their own wine at the college."

"If the others do it, we wouldn't want him to be without," she said apologetically.

"Indeed no. It is kind of you, and I shall thank you as it is by no means sure Tom will remember to."

They exchanged a forgiving smile at Tom's thoughtless ways. It did not occur to either of them that a young man needs some discipline. Tom had had plenty of that when his papa was alive, and now he was at Oxford, beyond their daily supervision. Lettie had assumed he would return to Laurel Hall and set up as a squire when he graduated, but he had recently informed her that he meant to establish himself in London instead and take up politics.

They were exceedingly proud of him and agreed that it was only a matter of time till he was a member of the Cabinet, possibly even the prime minister. The only disappointment was that they would see so little of Tom. Still, they would have the pleasure of reading about him in the journals, entertaining his company when he came to the hall, and of course visiting him in London. One incidental effect of Tom's decision was that Lettie was no longer concerned about making a match. Her ten-thousand-pound dowry did not permit her to set up and run a creditable establishment. She had not liked to think of living with Tom and his wife, when Tom married, but now she would continue to be mistress of Laurel Hall indefinitely.

They drove into Ashford and did their business at the bank, then spent a very enjoyable hour selecting a shawl and a few gewgaws for the spring assembly. Lettie had planned to have new white kid gloves as well, but Tom's waistcoats took precedence. The gloves would be reduced in price after the assembly, and she would have new ones for the autumn assembly instead. They rounded off the visit by taking lunch at the Royal Crown and enjoying a stroll through its famous gardens before returning home.

Chapter Two

A WEEK PASSED, bringing neither thanks from Tom for the gift nor further requests from Lord Havergal for money, but bringing a ten-pound leg of pork from Mr. Norton and, most importantly of all, bringing the spring assembly a week closer. Only two days away now, it colored every hour of every day. The days were not long enough for all the unguents Violet and Lettie wished to apply to their faces, the new hairdos to be tried, the washing of stockings, and the pressing of gowns.

They had other important matters to fill their hours as well. It was the custom at Laurel Hall to entertain a small party to dinner before the assembly. Due to Mr. Beddoes's death, the custom had lapsed last year, but this year Lettie was reinstituting it. To leave every servant free for the grand affair on Friday, she moved washing day up to Wednesday. On that Wednesday afternoon, Violet and Lettie sat in the gold saloon, fatigued at four o'clock from the exertions of preparing for the dinner party and checking up on the washing.

The washing was nominally in Cook's charge, who took all household matters under her capable hands. Mrs. Siddons (wife of the butler) ought, by

12

rights, to be called a housekeeper, but as she ruled from the kitchen and refused to dress for the grander role, she maintained her more humble title of Cook. Up to her elbows in advance preparations for the dinner party, she told Lettie she would be serving cold ham and bread pudding for dinner. Lettie told her that was fine.

Emboldened by success, Cook next informed her mistress that she must keep an eye on Bess with the laundry, and Miss Beddoes did as she was told. It was best not to vex this irreplaceable jewel, especially when her cooperation was required for the important dinner party. Lettie had made half a dozen trips downstairs to see Bess wasn't letting the new washing dolly "eat" her sheets and tablecloths. This new cannibal contrivance possessed two sturdy wooden paddles, which Bess moved by an attached handle. If she was not careful, the laundry wedged its way under the paddles and was stirred into rags.

Lettie had just returned to the saloon when there was a rattle of wheels on the driveway. "Mr. Norton!" Violet exclaimed, patting her brown curls in pleasure. Lettie arranged a lukewarm smile to greet him. Before Siddons could shuffle to the door, the knock came, loud and importunate. "He sounds strangely perturbed," Violet said. "I hope nothing is amiss."

"Oh Lord, I hope his pigs haven't got into the roadway again. They upset a dung cart last time."

Siddons was surprised at the vehemence of the knocker, too, and shuffled faster to open the door.

Into the waiting silence came the sound of a young male voice, full of authority and self-consequence. "Lord Havergal," the voice said. "I am here to see Mr. Beddoes. Is he in?"

"He doesn't live here," Siddons said. He was perfectly familiar with Lord Havergal's name but unaware of the identity of the current Mr. Beddoes.

"What the devil are you talking about? I had a letter from him yesterday. I told him I was coming."

"But he's at Oxford—a student."

"Ah, that explains the error. I wish to see his father."

"He's dead."

"Now listen, my good man," the voice continued, rising in impatience now, but still good natured. "Dead men don't write letters, do they? Quit joshing me, and tell Beddoes I am here."

There darted into Lettie's head an image of the latest cartoon of Lord Havergal, and she felt very much inclined to swoon. Lord Havergal, and he wanted to see her! Her next futile thought was of escape, but that arrogant voice was adamant. It would find her if she ran and hid in a trunk in the attic. She rose on shaking knees and went to the door. "Pray show Lord Havergal in, Siddons," she said, peering to see the owner of that arrogant voice.

The breath caught in her lungs, and she found herself staring like any country bumpkin. The cartoons had not done him justice, but they had caught the essence of Lord Havergal. The jaw was not quite so ludicrously large and square, the shoulders not quite as broad as a barn door, but the overall effect was of an exceedingly well-built, handsome, elegant gentleman. And here was she, in her shabbiest gown, with her hair falling about her ears, haggard from running upstairs and downstairs to check the laundry. It was not losing his admiration that galled her, but that he should see her in such tawdry disarray. Had she had a choice, she would have been wearing her most daunting and matronly gown.

The vision stepped forward, handing Siddons his curled beaver and shucking off his drab driving coat to reveal a jacket of blue Bath cloth that fit so well, it seemed like a second skin. Beneath it he wore a flowered waistcoat. A pair of dancing blue eyes met Lettie's glance, and a spontaneous smile flashed out to devastate her. No mere mortal had such a smile. The man was either devil or angel. Havergal advanced, hand extended to grip hers in a firm shake.

"There is some mistake obviously," he said with a charming bow. "Is this not Laurel Hall?"

"It is," she said weakly, and pulled her hand away.

He advanced toward the gold saloon door. "Your butler is addlepated. He must have got into the wine," he said, but with no air of accusation. She let this calumny against her abstemious butler pass without a word. "I have come to see Mr. Beddoes," he announced, and waited for her reply.

"There is—that is—I—*I* am Mr. Beddoes," she said, and felt a pink flush suffuse her cheeks. On the sofa Violet emitted a squeak not unlike that of a cornered mouse.

Into the silence came the slight squawk of a poorly oiled hinge as Siddons closed the front door. Havergal stared at her, speechless. His questioning glance suggested this was some kind of hoax or joke. His handsome features soon eased into a smile as he decided to jolly her along. She might have influence with old Beddoes, he thought. Who could she be? A lady, certainly, though not the sort of lady *I* am accustomed to. He raked her in quick scrutiny from head to toe and said, "One would never guess it to look at you, Mr. Beddoes." He smiled and glanced at Violet. "And this would be your—brother?" he asked archly.

It was at that moment that Violet fell in love with Lord Havergal. His blue eyes looked deeply into hers, seeming to share some joke. She *did* like a man with a sense of humor, which just goes to prove the old saw that opposites attract. She tittered coyly and looked at Lettie.

"My companion, Miss FitzSimmons," she said stiffly. "Pray, have a seat, Lord Havergal." He went to the sofa and sat beside Violet, who later told Miss Beddoes that she felt a tremor in her heart at the proximity.

Again those blue eyes directed a beam at Lettie, asking for some explanation. "You haven't told me your name, ma'am," he said.

"I am Miss Beddoes."

"Ah, then my guardian is your father, I take it?"

"He—he was. Papa passed away a year ago. I succeeded him in the will as testamentary guardian in the trust."

He blinked twice. "But you're a *lady*!" he said, stunned.

"Yes."

"This can't be legal!" A bright gleam of hope flashed in his eyes. He suspected there was something havey-cavey afoot here. It was unusual for a lady to be guardian to a grown man—even illegal, or why try to hide it? Immediately it darted into his head that he could upset the trust and get his whole twenty-five thousand.

"I assure you it is perfectly legal," she said firmly. "The solicitors examined the matter thoroughly." She spoke with the confidence of knowledge, hoping that the proud set of her head left no doubt about it.

Havergal was much inclined to argue, but caution suggested keeping on good terms till he had a word with his own solicitor. "Well, it is very strange," he said, frowning.

"Yes, but not unheard of for mothers or aunts to

be guardians of children." He bristled. "Not that I mean to say you are a child!" she added hastily.

He examined her face for signs of age. The lady was no spring lamb, but she didn't look forty or anything like it. Her flesh was still firm, and her eyes were clear. "Not quite so—mature as yourself perhaps," he said ingratiatingly, and was rewarded with a gimlet shot from a pair of angry gray eyes. Thirty-five, he decided, old enough to be tender about her years. "But perfectly competent, I'm sure," he added.

"Kind of you to say so. Your cousin Horace did not think me *incompetent* at least."

"Was it his idea for you to pretend you were a man?" he asked in confusion.

"No indeed. I never pretended I was. I signed my letters L. A. Beddoes. It was yourself who assumed I was a man."

"I'm sorry," he said, and shook his head. He couldn't believe he was apologizing. The witch had led him astray on purpose all these months.

Miss Beddoes nodded her absolution. "Were you just in the neighborhood, Lord Havergal, or did you come on purpose to visit me?"

"Did you not have my note?" he asked, surprised.

"Not a word since your request for an advance. You *did* receive my reply?"

"Yes, but I wrote you again that I would come in person."

"When did you write this?"

"Yesterday."

"Then I expect I shall receive it tomorrow morning. The post is not so fast as your carriage, it seems."

He disliked the condescension of that speech but held in his annoyance. "Another matter has come up—a business matter that I would like to discuss with you—though I daresay a lady wouldn't appreciate the *marvelous* opportunity. It seems a shame to lose out on it when the money is just sitting there."

She leveled a cool look at him. "A pity Hamlet let you down, or you might have used the thousand pounds you lost on that race in Green Park."

Violet emitted another muted squeak, as though to disassociate herself from the charge. Havergal felt like a schoolboy in the schoolmaster's office. He squared his shoulders and said, "This has nothing to do with gambling debts. It is business, pure and simple. I should think the very least you would do is listen to what I have to say."

"Does this business opportunity guarantee you more than five percent? Is it backed by the government of England?"

"Of course not! Consols at five percent hardly constitute an *opportunity*. They are for little old ladies who—" She shot him a glare that reduced his confidence to cinders. He came to an embarrassed pause before stumbling on. "For people who are afraid to take a risk."

"People like guardians, who are not expected to risk their charge's money. I must refuse—once again. Would you care for a glass of wine before leaving, Lord Havergal?" Lettie congratulated herself on her restraint. Little old ladies, indeed!

His resolution firmed, and he said, "We haven't got this matter settled yet."

"On the contrary, it *is* settled, milord. I will not advance you any money for a venture that might lose the whole."

"You haven't even heard what I have to say! This is a marvelous opportunity. A new scientific technique that will revolutionize—"

"If it is so marvelous as that, appeal to your father. He holds the majority of your funds, does he not?"

"Papa is so old-fashioned, he doesn't realize the world is changing."

"If your own father is against the investment, you cannot expect me to authorize it."

For sixty seconds he sat glaring at her in frustration. Violet took pity on him and said, "I shall ring Siddons for the wine."

While the butler served wine, Havergal assumed an air of concentration, trying to regroup his thoughts and come up with some tale to con this Turk. He sensed that Miss FitzSimmons was already in love with him and might prove an ally. He turned and smiled at her. "This glass of wine is excellent and very welcome after my long drive," he said. "I hadn't thought it would take me four hours to come from London." His eyes darted to Miss Beddoes. If the woman had blood in her veins, and not ice water, she must invite him to dinner at least.

"Four hours! It takes us eight, which is why we never go. You must have flown!" Violet said, vastly impressed and mindless of the fact that she had just painted the ladies of Laurel Hall as deep-dyed provincials. It was only confirmation of what their toilettes had already told him.

"I drove my curricle. My grays make pretty good time," he said nonchalantly.

"Oh my. I have never been in a sporting carriage. They look very lively when one sees them coursing along the road."

"I must take you for a spin before I leave."

"Your horses must be fagged to death," Violet said, disappointed to lose out on the trip.

"They'll be fine by morning. I shall put up at the inn in town tonight and return tomorrow morning. Perhaps you can suggest a good place to dine?"

Violet directed a meaningful stare at Lettie, who stared back unmoved. She felt not an iota of pity for Havergal, but she did value the honor of having noble connections and made the expected offer. "Perhaps you would dine with us, Lord Havergal?" she asked coldly.

"That's very kind of you." All I had to do was sit up and beg! he thought slyly. "I would be delighted, Miss Beddoes. My valet should be arriving soon with my evening clothes. He is following in my carriage—no room in my curricle for more than my groom."

She stared in consternation. What was all this about valets and carriages and grooms? Was he planning to make an extended stay? It was wash day, and they were only having ham and bread pudding. She was on pins and needles till the wine was drunk, and Havergal expressed an interest in taking a walk through the park to stretch his legs.

"Could I induce you to accompany me, Miss Beddoes?" he asked, forcing a smile on his handsome face. He hoped that in some romantic setting, away from other eyes, he might try a little flirtation and soften her stiff demeanor. Ladies were becoming desperate by five and thirty. She wasn't wearing a cap, so she hadn't despaired of marrying some unfortunate soul.

"I'm afraid I am busy, Lord Havergal." She'd have to speak to Cook and the upstairs maid to see that the best guest suite was dusted. Havergal would have to change his clothes.

Violet realized the upheaval facing her friend and watched with sad eyes as Havergal left the saloon alone. She would have liked to offer to accompany him.

"Long threatening has come at last," she said, and smiled fatuously. "I mean Havergal's discovering you are a lady. Isn't he handsome, Lettie? I never saw anyone so good-looking, just like a hero in a play or a novel."

"He's a handsome enough scoundrel," she admitted reluctantly, "which is not to say he is going to con me into giving him the money to bet on a pig race."

"You could have listened to what he had to say at least."

"If his father wouldn't approve of the scheme, why should I?"

Violet had nothing to say about that. "Imagine, Lettie. We are dining with a viscount. I might almost say 'The Viscount,' for I am sure he is the most talked-about man in London."

"Yes, and we will be serving this highly polished article bread pudding, unless I go and speak to Cook. You see to the bedchamber, and I'll run down to the kitchen. I hope Cook will let us have a cake and get hold of some fowl—a goose or a couple of chickens—to eke out that ham." She went belowstairs.

Lettie took a peek through the window later as they rustled about their errands, and in the park, she saw Havergal "stretching his legs" on a rock with his head in his hands. He looked bored to flinders already. He'd rather sit alone staring at the ground than be in this house. How he must despise them—her. It did not seem this day could possibly get any worse, but she was mistaken.

Cook came in and announced with ill-concealed glee, "The washing dolly chewed the lace of your best petticoat. Bess turns the wheel too hard. I told you so." That would teach them to go ordering up fine dinners on short notice and at such a busy time.

"I'd best go and have a look."

This was a mere annoyance to Lettie. A greater annoyance was soon added on top of it. While she was belowstairs, Siddons came pelting down with a large brown parcel in his hands and said, "Norton's here. Another demmed suckling pig, and us with two in the larder already. He's upstairs waiting for you with Lord Havergal, Miss Beddoes."

"We should set up a butcher shop," Cook grumbled, and disposed of the brown package.

Lettie could think of no friend she was more reluctant to introduce to Lord Havergal than Mr. Norton. What could those two possibly have in common? Lord Havergal would place her on a social plateau with the pig farmer, and Norton would be prosing poor Lord Havergal's ear off with talk of farrowing, breeding, and lard bellies.

"Will Norton be staying to eat, too?" Cook demanded fiercely.

"I shall let you know as soon as I find out."

She sent off for Violet and went upstairs reluctantly.

Chapter Three

"IT IS ALL a sham," Norton's unpolished tones informed Lord Havergal. Lettie could hear him in the hall, five yards away. It sounded like an accusation. For one frightening moment she thought Norton had strayed from his favorite subject, one might almost say his only subject, but she was mistaken. "I never knew a sow to eat her young," he continued. "She might roll over on them. That will finish them when the porkers are newborn, still in the farrowing pen. No sir, it is your boars you have to keep a sharp eye on. They are very testy at farrowing time. And who are almost worse are your gilts."

"Ah yes, the gilts," Havergal said in a voice of utter bewilderment.

"I have two dozen of them. You must pop over to Norton Knoll—but my wits are gone begging. Norton Knoll is my *hop* farm. I raise hops as well as swine. Perhaps you saw my hop farm as you approached from Ashford? A great Norman heap? My pig farm, my swinery I call it—heh, heh—is further south."

She dashed quickly in to rescue Lord Havergal. Both gentlemen leapt to their feet. After a polite pretense at pleasure in seeing Norton, she said, "Miss FitzSimmons will be with us shortly."

While Havergal gave a graceful but casual bow, Norton bent from the waist with a jerk, like a clockwork figure. All Norton's efforts at being a gentleman were similarly stiff and overdone. His brown hair was plastered with some substance that held it in perfectly immobile waves. His ruddy complexion was incapable of subduing. It glowed, as did his brown eyes. As to the rest of his face, he was not so much ugly as plain. His nose had no real shape, but just sat there as a buffer between eyes and lips. On those rare occasions when his lips were still, they were thin. For calling at Laurel Hall or going to the village, he dressed in the very height of provincial fashion, with tight-fitting jackets, extravagant cravats, and flowery waistcoats. His figure was substantial but not fat, despite the quantity of fresh pork that nourished it.

He said, "Ah, g'day, Miss Lettie. You are looking lovely, as usual." Then in the blinking of an eye, he was back on his hobbyhorse and trying to get Havergal to join him. "Young Lord Havergal was just telling me he is keen on pigs."

"How nice," she said weakly.

"It is something all the world has in common, when you come down to it," Norton continued. "We of the more fortunate class—"with an encompassing smile he included both listeners in this privileged few—"like our gammon and ham and pork. The servants take kindly to a pig's face or a boiled foot. Why, the Krauts even eat the tails. For my own house, Miss Millie figures them good for nothing but making a broth."

"How is your sister, Mr. Norton?" Lettie interjected hastily, hoping to divert him. Norton lived with his older sister, Millicent. He had no other sister but still denied her the honor of being Miss

24

Norton. She was Miss Millie to all the county, and under his aegis, Miss Beddoes and Miss Fitz-Simmons were being similarly lowered.

"In fine fettle. She was out straightening the pea sticks when I left," he said, and returned at once to his subject. "I used to raise lard pigs. They are great, ungainly creatures. Now I am into fresh pork. The carcass is lighter than your lard pig, but not so long and lean as your bacon pig. A good fresh pork carcass is one hundred pounds deadweight."

"Really!" Havergal exclaimed with simulated interest.

Violet joined them and was complimented on looking "lovely as usual," before Norton took up his theme again. Havergal made the error of asking what breed he raised and was told in detail.

"Crossbreeding is the thing. I am part of the movement to establish the Berkshire breed. I find your Yorkshire boar makes a dandy sire to an Essex, Large Black, or Cornwall sow. The Cornwall has good mothering qualities. But as to racing pigs, I should think you'd want to stick to your bacon pig for that, Lord Havergal. They are lighter and livelier. Your boar would outrun your sow, of course."

Havergal shot a guilty peep in Lettie's direction. She saw that he had brought this lecture on himself and gave up feeling sorry for him. His guilt soon turned to laughter, and he said, "I see by your black frowns you have misunderstood the matter, Miss Beddoes. I am not thinking of racing the bacon boars myself, but raising them as a new breed to make money, as one raises Thoroughbreds."

Norton was all ears. "Do you think it will catch on at all—in a big way, I mean? I am always looking out for a new wrinkle of this sort. I know of a dandy Chester White that is going up to auction. Their legs are a little longer than most, I think. Mate her with a highbred bacon boar—"

"A nick of the right bloodlines." Havergal nodded, reverting, in his confusion, to horse-racing terminology. "If you will let me do myself the honor of calling on you, Mr. Norton, we shall discuss this further," he added with an apologetic glance at his hostess. He noticed that this subject was displeasing to her.

"Heh, heh. You need pay no heed to Miss Lettie," Norton assured him. "She always looks like a bear with a toothache, but it is just her way. Underneath it all, she is as kind a soul as you will meet."

Lettie ignored the quizzing smiles Havergal was shooting in her direction and looked instead at the long case clock in the corner. It was nearing six o'clock, their customary dinner hour. Norton, to do him justice, was never slow to take a hint. He was working on his manners and his accent, and his kind nature was a help in the former.

"You are wishing me at Jericho, Miss Lettie," he said bluntly. "I know when you begin slanting your eyes at the clock and drumming your fingers that you are ready for fork work. No doubt you are famished. You'll want to run upstairs and change into your finery for Lord Havergal. I shall be off now. I told Miss Millie I might dine at the inn," he added. This was his way of announcing he was not expected at home.

Lettie was in no mood to oblige him, but if she didn't, there would be hurt feelings. Violet made the expected offer. "Lord Havergal's luggage has not arrived, and we are all dining in our afternoon clothes, so you must join us," she said. He agreed without so much as a murmur of demur.

"You talked me into it. Very kind I'm sure."

"You may regret it," Lettie warned him, though her real reason was to let Havergal know she usually set a better table. "We are serving potluck.

26

This is wash day, and the servants have been un-usually busy."

"No need for excuses, lass. The company is the thing," he said forgivingly, and added, "I can al-ways fill up at home."

When the expected call came from Siddons, Nor-ton seized Lettie's arm and hustled her off to the dining room at top speed. Things there were as fine as the prevailing conditions made possible. A bou-quet of early blooms culled from the garden formed a centerpiece for the table. The best linen cloth was in place, and the china and silverware were unex-ceptionable.

"If we had known you were coming, we would have had a fish course," Violet explained to the guests.

"Everything is very nice," Havergal assured her. "It is I who should apologize, barging in unan-nounced."

Norton scrutinized the sideboard more closely than a dinner guest should and pulled the chair to Lettie's right hand for himself. Havergal pretended not to notice and sat on her left.

Norton did not speak when he was eating. It was a lingering trait of his less affluent days. He gob-bled up his food as if he might not see more for a week. Violet decided the potatoes were overdone, and Havergal insisted they were just like he liked them. They took turns apologizing and explaining till Lettie was tired of it all.

"Let us agree dinner is a mess and speak of some-thing else," she said irritably.

Havergal murmured a quiet "Amen." He waited to hear what subject she might raise, but as she cut into a bird as tough as white leather and began chewing determinedly, he saw that the enlivening of the conversation was up to him.

"Do you hunt, Miss Lettie?" he asked.

"No, I have never hunted."

"Do you ride at all?"

"A little. My mount is getting old."

"Lettie says she and Ruby are growing old together," Violet told him. "When Ruby is past it, then Lettie means to quit riding altogether."

Lettie gave her a sharp glare. Havergal caught it and bit back a smile. So Miss Lettie *was* tender about her age, as he suspected. "How old is Ruby, Miss Lettie?" he asked. He purposely used Norton's way of addressing her, as it sounded more friendly.

"She is eighteen."

"Then she will surely beat you to retirement." He smiled. "It is generally held that a horse of twenty is the equivalent of a man of seventy. I cannot believe that a young lady like yourself, in the prime of life, will be ready for pasture in two years."

Nor was she quite ready for condescending assurances of this sort. "I haven't ordered up my Bath chair yet," she said.

Norton glanced up from his eating and said, "Ho, Bath chair! That is a good one, Miss Lettie. You ought to see her pelting along the meadows, milord. Her shank's mare can outpace a racehorse."

"How long does a pig remain race-worthy, Lord Havergal?" Lettie snipped. "I am thinking, of course, of your Hamlet."

"I'm afraid I can't enlighten you, ma'am. The pig-racing business is new to me. Perhaps our eminent authority can inform us?" he said, turning to Norton.

Norton lifted his head from his plate long enough to say, "You ought to get ten years out of a healthy trotter."

Somehow or other the talk turned to Tom. "Miss Beddoes's brother, Tom, wants to take up politics when he comes down from university this spring," Violet mentioned.

"Indeed?" Havergal asked. "What university is he attending?"

"Christ Church, Oxford," Lettie replied.

Havergal, alert to her moods, noticed this was a subject dear to her heart. "Excellent! It is my own college. But you must not fear all the graduates are so worthless as I," he added with one of his infamous smiles.

It was a smile no woman under ninety years old could be entirely immune to. "At least he isn't reading pig racing," she allowed with a little unsteadiness of the lips that might be interpreted as a stillborn smile.

"He will not return to Laurel Hall when he graduates, then?" Havergal said.

"No, he has expressed interest in a political career."

"Will he stand for Parliament?"

"His plans are not firm yet, except that he means to go up to London and look for a position."

"I will be happy to arrange introductions for him, if that would help." He was rewarded with a definite smile. "Will you remain in Kent to look after the estate?" he asked.

"For the present," she said vaguely.

There was some softening of attitudes over the rest of dinner. As long as Havergal didn't mention money, he was safe, but he had come here to get his money, and the prickly topic could not be ignored forever. As he was staying in the vicinity for a day or two, however, there was no need to rush into it immediately.

"We shall leave you and Mr. Norton to your port," Lettie announced when dinner was over. The bread pudding did not detain anyone but Mr. Norton for long. Cook had not seen fit to oblige her mistress with a cake.

"Horn-and-hoof management, that is the way to

do it," Norton said approvingly when the unappetizing dish was set before him. "No need to waste stale bread and crusts when a handful of raisins and a sprinkle of cinnamon make them entirely edible." Lettie turned a deaf ear on his compliment.

"We'll take our port in the saloon as usual," Norton said, inferring he ran quite tame at Laurel Hall. "A man would be a fool to deny himself the pleasure of such lovely ladies' company. Lord Havergal will second me on that, eh laddie?"

Lord Havergal's eyebrows rose in astonishment. When they came back down he said, "Just as you wish," and rose to leave.

They had no sooner entered the saloon than there was a gentle tap at the front door. As the usual evening caller, Norton, was already with them, Lettie could not think who it might be.

The soft, sibilant sounds of a gentleman's voice were audible, but no words could be distinguished. Within seconds, Siddons appeared at the door and announced with great pomp, "His Grace, the Duke of Crymont."

A *duke*? No such person lived within a day's driving distance of Laurel Hall. An earl was the highest nobility in the parish, and old Lord Devere had never called on them in his life. Lettie was glad she hadn't yet taken a seat, for she was uncertain whether a lady was expected to rise for a duke. Violet looked ready to faint, and Norton stood with his mouth hanging open in astonishment. All three looked to the doorway with the liveliest curiosity. Lettie had not expected a duke to be so small, but in all other details he fulfilled every expectation of ducal grandeur.

His Grace wore proper evening attire. He was a perfect model of noble elegance, from the gloss of his chestnut curls to the sheen of his patent-leather slippers, not omitting a black evening suit, immaculate cravat, and a ruby the size of a cherry inserted in the latter. He shimmered forward and took Lettie's hand, not to shake, but to raise to within an inch of his lips for a kiss.

"Madam," he said in hushed tones. "I am honored." He then lifted his little head, tossed it in Siddons's direction, and reached out his hand to receive what Siddons was holding. It was a bouquet of roses. He took it and handed it to her.

"Why thank you, sir," she said, blinking in confusion.

It soon came out that Havergal was the cause of this strange visit. "Crymont, allow me to present Miss Lettie Beddoes," he said, and went on to include the others. "The duke is on his way home to Havenhurst from London and mentioned he might stop at Ashford."

"I would have been here sooner, but I was held up by a rush of callers and did not arrive till six. I took dinner at the inn and came along as soon as possible."

Lettie thought it strange that the duke should be calling on Havergal at Laurel Hall. Was he under the misapprehension that Havergal was staying here? Worse, did Havergal himself expect an offer of rack and manger? She gave Siddons the flowers and sent him off to put them in a vase.

The visit had one good effect. It turned Norton into a mute. He said not a word but just stared at every detail of the duke's toilette. When he had learned who the duke was and that he was here to see Havergal, he ran off home to tell the news to Miss Millie, who would soon relay it to the whole town.

Violet remembered her manners and said, "Perhaps everyone would like to have tea now—or would you prefer port?"

31

"A cup of tea would be marvelous," Crymont decided.

Tea was called for, and the four mismatched people took up seats to await its arrival. "So, Havergal, were you shocked to discover 'old Beddoes' is a lady?" Crymont asked with an arch look at his hostess. "I was told at the inn, madam, when I was seeking directions here, that you are Havergal's guardian."

"I was surprised," Havergal admitted.

"He was shocked," Lettie said to the duke.

"Why did you play such a stunt on the poor boy?" Crymont demanded, and she gave her explanation.

"Well, it is an odd thing," Crymont said consideringly, "but by no means unique. My cousin Jethro had his bit of blunt left in the hands of his sister, for he was a wastrel. Not to say that Havergal is one!" he added swiftly.

"No indeed," she agreed demurely.

Havergal felt his spirits sink. He had thought there might be a legal way out of this position, but his friend's word convinced him otherwise.

The tea arrived, and Lettie poured for the guests.

"What sort of a town is Ashford?" Crymont asked. "Do they have assemblies and things?"

"Indeed we do," Violet told him. "There will be a spring assembly on Friday evening."

"Friday? That is only two days away. We must stick around for that, Havergal," he said in a perfectly bored tone at odds with his speech. "Perhaps we can induce the ladies to accompany us?" he asked with as close as he ever came to a smile in Violet's direction.

"I hadn't planned to stay quite that—" Havergal began.

"We might as well," Crymont said, and drew a weary sigh. "London is dull as ditch water this week, which is why I left. There is nothing new playing at any of the theaters. We've seen the offerings at both Drury Lane and Covent Garden. There is only Castlereagh's ball and Mrs. Johnston's rout, and of course Gully's ridotto. Oh, and I believe Lady Eskott asked us to dinner, but Auntie won't mind if we shab off."

Lettie's mind reeled to think of so many entertainments. What had Ashford to offer? It was pure chance that the spring assembly was coming up. Other than that, it would be dinner with the vicar and friends and perhaps a few calls from Mr. Norton. Almost certainly a barrage of calls from Norton with the spring assembly looming. Wouldn't she love to appear at that assembly on Havergal's arm!

"Oh my," Violet said. "Ashford has nothing like that to offer."

"One comes to the country to rusticate," Crymont informed her wearily. "Is it a firm date for the assembly, ladies? Havergal?" He looked from one to the other. Havergal sat, undecided.

"We certainly plan to attend," Violet said. "I hope you will remain and come with us."

"That will be delightful," Havergal said reluctantly. He looked far from delighted and sounded miserable.

"Then it's settled," Crymont said with quiet satisfaction. "And tomorrow evening you ladies must let Havergal and me take you to dinner at the Royal Oak. They do a splendid baron of beef." His head turned toward Lettie. "You will have some suggestion where we can go for a drive in the afternoon, Miss Beddoes?" An inflection on the last words made it a question.

A holiday in the company of a duke and an exceedingly handsome viscount was too much temptation. Instead of the cool facade she had planned to present, she replied civilly, "Canterbury is not very far away."

"Ah, I should drop in on Uncle Clarence—the archbishop," he added for their edification.

"Oh my," Violet whispered. Her face wore the dazed look it wore when she was reading one of her marble-covered novels.

Crymont drank up his tea rather quickly and set down his cup. "This has been delightful, but I really must be running along. Havergal, I know, is putting up with you, but I have booked rooms at the Royal Oak. At what hour will it be convenient for me to call tomorrow, madam?"

Havergal writhed in embarrassment. "I am not putting up here," he said crossly.

"Oh do," Violet exclaimed. "We have had the bedchamber specially aired. There is no need for you to rush off."

Before answering, he looked hopefully at Lettie. Unable to make up her mind whether to encourage this scheme, she just looked away. "If you're sure it is no trouble. . . ."

Violet smiled, and it was settled.

Lettie said to Crymont, "Will two-thirty tomorrow be convenient, Your Grace?" She never thought she would be using such words as "Your Grace." Yet to tell the truth, the duke seemed less impressive than the viscount.

"Excellent."

After bows and curtsies were exchanged, Crymont left. Havergal accompanied him to the front door, trying to give a casual look to this new fashion. The ladies were highly curious as to what they were saying. By changing her chair, Lettie could see the leave-taking, but not hear it.

Siddons appeared with His Grace's many-collared driving cape and curled beaver. Crymont permitted him to help him on with his vestments, then left with a silent wink at his friend. There was a world of mischief in that wink, yet Lettie could not believe Havergal had actually arranged the visit. His expression was one of surprise when Crymont arrived. Havergal looked mystified at that moment, but he schooled his features to blandness before returning to the gold saloon.

When he had first followed Crymont out, Lettie had allowed herself one angry "Encroaching! One would think he was the host, following Crymont to the door."

"Hush, Lettie. He'll hear you."

"I don't care if he does. I can be rude, too. I shall take up the journal and read when he comes back."

Upon his return she sat with her nose in the paper. The habit of good manners proved hard to break, however, and she soon lowered the paper.

"Don't let me disturb you if you wish to read, Miss Lettie," he said politely.

She made some initial demur, but when Violet engaged him in talk—gossip really—about Crymont, she resumed her "reading," which did not prevent her from overhearing every word of their conversation. She learned that the Duke of Crymont was extremely rich and heard some details about his estates, but in the ensuing half hour, she did not learn one fact that reflected credit on his character. He was fortunate to have inherited so much, he had pretty manners, he was tolerably handsome, and when one said that, one had said it all.

In short, he was cut from the same bolt as Havergal. They were lucky, but they were not particularly worthwhile. The duke's higher titles and larger fortune were countered by Havergal's striking appearance and more engaging personality. It was unusual and gratifying to have two such noblemen calling on them, especially with the assembly so near, but they must not lose track of why they were calling. Havergal wanted more money to waste, and Crymont, she suspected, was abetting him.

At the end of thirty minutes, Havergal gave a polite stretch and said, "I must not keep you ladies up too late. Not that you need any beauty sleep," he added gallantly.

"Oh, you are retiring?" Lettie said, lowering her paper.

"It was a fagging trip." Eager to ingratiate her, he rose and glanced at what he was reading. "What is it that has captured your interest so keenly, Miss Lettie?"

She peered up from the paper and found herself being studied by a pair of sparkling eyes, fringed with enviable lashes. The cartoons had not exaggerated that feature much. She glanced hastily at a headline and said, "I was just reading about the new Apothecaries Act, which is going to forbid unqualified doctors from practicing medicine."

"And a good thing, too," he declared. "There are too many quacks and bloodletters hanging up their shingles. What will be the criteria for qualification?"

She quickly scanned the column. "Applicants will have to pass an examination set by the Society of Apothecaries. Would you like to read the article, Lord Havergal?"

"If you're sure you're through with it."

"Quite sure." She folded up the paper and handed it to him. It was an invitation for him to leave. He perched on the edge of the sofa and looked at the paper. "Have you noticed the print in the *Times* is clearer than it used to be last year?"

"*I* noticed it," Violet said at once. "Don't you remember we discussed it, Lettie? I was complaining of needing spectacles, then the *Times* suddenly seemed easier to read."

"They switched to a steam-powered press last November," Havergal told them. He needed a pretext for wanting money and had chosen an investment in the new steam press. He had swotted up on it and wanted to deliver his lecture.

"Fancy that," Violet said.

"It prints eleven hundred sheets an hour—they think they can get it up to eighteen hundred. Two hundred and fifty an hour is considered pretty good by the handpress. Konig, a German fellow, devised the system. It will be adopted by book printers as well. The makers of those dreadful marble-covered novels will have us buried under a blanket of swooning heroines and wicked villains."

Violet smiled weakly. A reply was up to Lettie, and she said, "You leave out the most important character, sir. Pray do not forget the hero. That, I fancy, is why the ladies read those books. At least it is why *I* do," she added with a challenging look.

Havergal made an exaggerated grimace. "Pause while I unwedge my foot from my mouth, ladies. No disparagement was intended, I promise you. I read a deal of tripe myself." He hastily scanned his mind for any light reading he had glanced at recently and said, "Walter Scott, for example. I adore him." Their surprised faces suggested that Scott was considered pretty heavy stuff, and he looked lower. "Lewis's *The Monk*, and Walpole's *Castle of Otranto*," he added.

"Surely you are not calling *Otranto* tripe!" Violet exclaimed.

"Oh well, but *good* tripe," he said, and laughed at his own foolishness.

There was something infectious in his laughter. Lettie found herself smiling. "As opposed to bad tripe, like Plato," she riposted. "I was never so taken in in my life as when I opened Tom's copy of *The Republic*, expecting to become wise. I turned first, of course, to the bit on 'Women and the Family.' As soon as I read that one sex—and you need not ask which one—is much better at *everything* than the other, I tossed the book aside."

"Yet he is more lenient toward women than many philosophers," Havergal said mischievously.

"Then you have just saved me the bother of reading the others. What I especially despised was that cipher, Glaucon, with his interminable 'certainly' and 'exactly' and 'agreed.' I could just imagine him, tugging his forelock and simpering."

Havergal firmed his tentative position on the edge of the sofa and said, "Philosophy, you know, is not really about the comparative worth of men and women. It is concerned with broader questions regarding the meaning of life, in the here and hereafter."

"I found no illumination there either, milord. As to eternity, your Plato begs the question. He does not prove that we have a soul but says categorically the soul cannot die because its own specific evil cannot kill it. An arbitrary statement, to say the least."

"I agree," he said. And added facetiously, tugging at a lock, "I'll be your Glaucon in this case. Plato was never one of my own favorite philosophers. He is too old, too far removed from our modern times. Have you read Kant, Miss Beddoes?"

"I've never heard of him," she said bluntly.

"You must let me send you a copy of his work."

They talked for ten minutes, till Havergal felt he had begun to philosophize a wedge into her opposition. He then took the newspaper to retire to his room. "This nice clear print will make night reading easy," he said. He bowed and left.

"He seems very nice," Violet said.

"I was surprised to find him interested in philosophy."

"And the duke—charming. A little on the small side, of course. I am thinking of the assembly."

"They are a pair of rogues, Violet. Havergal had Crymont come along to urge me to loosen the purse strings. He thinks I would be afraid to say no to a duke, but he is very much mistaken. I am going to tell Cook we shan't be home for dinner tomorrow evening. But the next evening, I think we must invite the duke and Havergal to our dinner party for the assembly."

"Oh my," Violet said with a beatific smile.

Chapter Four

"A BIT EARLY for the feather tick," Cuttle said to his master when Havergal entered his bedchamber.

Havergal's valet served double duty as a bruiser His Lordship was backing. Cuttle took his valeting duties lightly. He had the well-formed body and misshapen nose of his profession, along with a fine head of blond hair and blue eyes.

"I'm not going to bed. I'm going out as soon as the ladies retire," Havergal replied.

"On the sly, eh? Shall I pass the word along to Crooks?"

"Yes, and no, respectively."

"Eh?"

"Yes, on the sly; and no, I shan't require my groom. Crymont is driving me. Questions might arise if my carriage leaves the stable."

"Where are you going?"Cuttle demanded in the easy tone of an equal.

"None of your business. Just slip downstairs after the others have retired, and see the door's left on the latch for me to get back in before morning."

"Laurel Hall ain't the kind of house you should be pulling off such stunts. You know Beddoes is a

40

crusty old devil. And provincial ladies—they'll take a dim view of petticoat dealings."

"You're letting that lascivious imagination of yours run away with you, Cuttle. Who said anything about petticoat dealings?"

"The duke—what else would it be?"

Havergal ignored him. "Run downstairs, and see if you can find out when the ladies retire."

"Eleven. I've already been."

"Damn, it's only ten. Crymont will have an hour to wait. I shall go now and slip out the window."

He went to the window, raised it, and looked for means of descent. No convenient vine clambered up the wall, but by climbing out and grasping onto Cuttle's outstretched arms, his feet came close enough to the ground that he figured he could drop without breaking an ankle. Within minutes he hit the soft earth unharmed and hastened toward the roadway.

He soon spotted a dark hulk in the shadows ahead where Crymont's carriage had pulled off the side of the road. "What kept you?" Crymont demanded in his usual petulant tone.

"I had to do the pretty with the ladies." Havergal climbed into the carriage, and Crymont pulled the check string to be off. "What made you decide to come?"

"I decided to add my beseechments to yours. A comely lady, Miss Beddoes," Crymont said.

"She's a Turk. It won't be easy bringing her around my thumb, but I have two ideas. Any mention of her brother brings a smile to her lips."

"Sure sign of a lady without a man in her life. And the other?"

"She fancies herself a bluestocking," he replied with a curl to his lips. This was no compliment. Both gentlemen preferred their ladies unspoiled by education. "She has misread a little Plato and enjoys to boast of it. I'll dump the butter boat on her vast learning and see if that won't do the trick. I only require a thousand. Damn that Hamlet!"

"She's a lady when all's said and done. Win her by wooing."

"And end up shackled for life? Thank you, no. Now to more interesting matters. Where are we off to?"

"The Royal Oak."

"I was hoping for a cockfight in some rural barn. I can't show my *phiz* at the inn. Word might get back to Laurel Hall."

"Live dangerously," Crymont urged in a voice of utter ennui. "The prize is worth the risk."

Havergal looked up, interested. "Cards?"

"It's a surprise, but you'll like it, I promise you."

"I can't afford to risk losing more blunt at this time."

"This is my treat, Havergal. It won't cost you a sou. No one will see us slip up to my room. The patrons will all be in the taproom at this hour."

Havergal allowed himself to be talked into this surprise, feeling it would be dinner and champagne, both of which would be welcome after the meager hospitality of Laurel Hall. The only person who saw them enter was the proprietor. Crymont, as usual, had taken the best suite at the inn. It was a double room with an adjoining door. Wine and four glasses were arranged on the dresser.

"From my own cellar," Crymont mentioned. "I left a case at Laurel Hall as well. It didn't seem an appropriate gift for the ladies, but the servants will appreciate it, so I gave it to the groom. One never knows when some extraordinary service will be required of servants."

"Kind of you. Who is joining us?" he asked, glancing at the four glasses.

Crymont allowed his boredom to slip into something bordering on excitement. "Havergal, you won't believe the luck. I talked Cherry Devereau into coming with me! She will *never* leave London, you must know. First time she's ever been outside the city. And we brought her friend with us, for you. A fetching redhead."

"Good God!" Havergal felt a strange ringing in his ears. He was temporarily bereft of oaths to express his anger and chagrin.

"You might well stare! The two prettiest bits of muslin in all of London. Who would have thought Cherry would come to—where are we? Ah yes, Ashford. It's costing me a pretty penny, I can tell you. Iona is so charming, I'm thinking of taking her under my protection as well when we return to town. Mind you don't breathe a word to Cherry."

"Crymont, you clunch! What's the matter with you, bringing lightskirts here at a time like this!" He paced the floor, raking his fingers through his hair. "Word of this will be all over town by morning. How often do you think Ashford sees a woman like Cherry Devereau?"

"Never! A rare treat for them, I fancy," he crowed.

"A treat? Try a scandal. I'm trying to pass for a pattern card of rectitude at Laurel Hall."

"We'll keep the girls under wraps. No one has seen them but the proprietor."

"Then the story is as good as published in the journals. I'm ruined. That's all. Ruined. I've got to get back to the house and make sure Miss Beddoes knows I'm there—all night."

"That sounds intriguing," Crymont said with a quizzing look. "Short of joining her in her bedchamber, how do you propose to accomplish that?"

"I'll think of something. I'm leaving. You'll have to lend me your carriage to return at once."

"But what of Iona?"

Havergal shot him a black look. "Let them sing a duet for you—then send them back to London."

"Singing wasn't what I had in mind."

"I know what you had in mind." At the door Havergal stopped a moment. "The redhead—Iona, did you say?"

"A lively wench with green eyes." Crymont pulled at his chin, waiting. "A full figure," he added enticingly, "and *very* friendly."

Havergal glared. "Send her off immediately! You must be mad." And so must he, for thinking he could stay for an hour without getting caught. He stomped out and slammed the door behind him. He sent for the groom and was soon ensconced in Crymont's well-sprung carriage, pondering how he could get back into the house. Not by the front door. The ladies wouldn't have retired yet. He could toss some pebbles at his own window and hope Cuttle heard him. . . .

He had the carriage stop some yards from the house and ran stealthily through the dark night the last length. As no light showed at his bedroom window, he assumed Cuttle was in the kitchen. Peering through that window, he saw Cuttle chatting to a female servant who was making bread. He'd stroll nonchalantly in through the back door and pretend he'd been at the stable. He'd give a sharp set-down if the servant inquired why he'd left by the front door and was returning by the back.

Cuttle turned a startled eye on him when he entered. Mrs. Siddons, in cap and apron, just glanced up, then returned to her dough.

"I went out to have a look at my grays," Havergal mentioned to Cuttle.

Cuttle, always eager to abet his master, said to Cook, "His Lordship is powerful fond of his bits o' blood."

"I'd like to see you upstairs, Cuttle," Havergal said.

He looked about for the the servants' stairs to avoid any chance of encounter with the ladies. When Cuttle rose, he stumbled against the table. Havergal flashed him a dangerous glare. Bosky! Damn his eyes. They were just approaching the staircase door when footsteps were heard, and Miss Beddoes came in at the other door. Havergal froze in his tracks.

"I wanted to have a word with you about breakfast, Cook," she said. Then she spotted Havergal and, like him, stood still, staring. "Lord Havergal!" she exclaimed.

Her shock was evident, and he rooted around in his mind for some explanation of his extraordinary behavior in invading her kitchen. His uppermost desire, however, was to establish firmly his innocence throughout the entire night. He said, "I was having trouble sleeping and came looking for a sleeping draft. Laudanum, or—" Yes, laudanum was the thing. How could he be carrying on with lightskirts when he was fast asleep? "Laudanum," he repeated more firmly.

"What is the trouble, headache?"

He snatched eagerly at this straw. "Yes, like a knife between my temples. Cuttle had already come below, or I would have sent him down," he added to forestall that question. From the corner of his eye he noticed Cuttle was weaving perilously. He moved his body into a position to conceal his valet.

"I have some headache powders," Lettie said.

Headache powders wouldn't prove he spent an innocent night asleep. "I would prefer laudanum. I never can sleep after one of these migraines."

Miss Beddoes was a firm lady but not without womanly compassion, and she could see that something was truly bothering Havergal. She said,

"Why don't you go up to bed? I don't keep laudanum in the house, but I'll send up some headache
powders."

"Very kind of you." Cuttle chose this moment to
lose his balance and bang against the edge of the
table. Lettie looked at him in alarm, and Havergal
spoke on in an attempt to cover the racket. "I'm
sorry to be such a nuisance, Miss Lettie."

"Not at all. It was the trip that did the mischief,
I expect. Travel is so very fatiguing, is it not? Perhaps you would like a posset as well? I find that
helpful for a sleepless night. I shall prepare it myself, from my own receipt, as Cook is in hands with
the bread."

"No, really, you are too kind, ma'am."

Havergal got Cuttle through the doors and on his
way upstairs, while Lettie assembled the pot and
her ingredients. When he was in his cups, Cuttle
liked to sing. He burst into raucous song as he
stumbled up the stairs. Lettie looked up from her
work and said, "I fear your valet has had something to drink, Lord Havergal."

"It sounds like it. And it's not the first time either. I shall ring a peel over him when I go upstairs. If this persists, I must turn him off," he said
stiffly.

The lecherous words of the song were indistinct
at least, and Havergal chattered on loudly to protect Miss Beddoes's maidenly ears. He felt that as
his hostess was being so obliging, it was his duty
to stay in the kitchen. He sat at the deal table opposite Cook, who was kneading her bread with
gusto, flour flying in the air as she punched it,
turned it over, and punched it again. He felt
wretched at his deceit and Miss Beddoes's kindness, and after all the trouble, a mere posset could
not prove he didn't wake up at midnight and dart
into town.

"I daresay this will put me out like a light," he said heartily, to plant this idea in her head.

"If you sleep poorly, stay in bed in the morning. If that headache persists, we shan't hold you to your promise of a drive."

"I wouldn't want to miss meeting the Archbishop of Canterbury," he said. Miss Beddoes lifted her eyes from the pot and gave him a long look. "It is not every day one has the honor of meeting an archbishop," he added inanely.

"That must be a very severe headache" is all she said, but it was enough to make him blush.

She poured the posset and handed it to him. "Do you have these headaches often, milord?"

"Frequently," he said, hoping to elicit sympathy.

"You must be doing something wrong. Trotting too hard, perhaps," she said with a conning smile. "And worrying about money. I daresay if you regularized your living, the headaches would disappear. I hope you sleep well."

"Thank you," he said through thin lips, and accepted the cup. He made a mechanical bow, not unlike Norton's, and left.

Cook lifted her flour-smudged face and said, "Headache. Hah! Hangover more like, if he sluices wine down like his valet. His Lordship came in by the back door, but he didn't leave by it. What was he doing at the stable if he had a headache?"

Lettie did not encourage her servants to gossip and did not mention that Havergal had not left by the front door either. How had he got out of the house? She reviewed her movements since his first going abovestairs, and she decided that he might have got out the front door when she and Violet went into the library to write the place cards for their dinner party. In any case, Havergal was not drunk like his valet. He had expressed the proper opinion in that matter.

In his room, Havergal ranted to Cuttle about the woman's demmed interfering manner. "Jawing at me, as if I were a schoolboy."

"What happened with the duke?" Cuttle asked.

"He had women at the inn. If she finds out, I'm sunk."

"How come you're home so early?"

"Don't be impertinent. Be sure to mention to Cook tomorrow that you were up half the night with me. I was here, *in this room* all night."

"Going out again then, are you?"

Havergal considered it a moment. He thought of a red-haired, green-eyed wench and was tempted, but in the end he said, "No, it ain't worth the risk. I'm tired as a racehorse anyway. Get rid of this slop, will you?" He handed the posset to Cuttle, who drank it off in one gulp.

"And while we're here, Cuttle, lay off the wine. You were staggering like a horse with the heaves. It won't do your boxing career any good, you know."

Cuttle gave a sheepish look. A hiccup prevented him from denying this charge, so he just backed away and left.

Havergal had a bottle of his own excellent wine and puzzled over the pages of his favorite philosopher, Kant. It was not an easy read, and he paid particular attention to some passages his father had underlined. His father had given him the book. Scanning these passages, Havergal read that the dignity of life did not depend on natural endowments, power, riches, or honor, but on goodwill. Intelligence, wit, judgment—all could be bad and mischievous if the character that makes use of them was not good.

What had Papa heard that he felt impelled to send him this sly message? Had he learned about Uncle Eustace's estate? Only three thousand guineas—the bequest had come at a particulary convenient time, just when he was overdrawn at the bank and had to settle up at Tatt's. Papa had expected him to give some portion of that money to the Cauleigh school for orphans. He should have sent a thousand at least. A thousand, Papa had mentioned earlier, would pay a teacher's salary for five years. Or it would pay for one bad race run by Hamlet. Did men actually live on two hundred guineas a year?

God, it must be awful to be poor. At the rate he was going, he would soon know. He really *must* curb his spending. But first he must pay his debts, and that meant charming Miss Beddoes into giving him an advance on his interest. Well, to be realistic, it meant biting into the capital left by Cousin Horace. Miss Beddoes could not give him unearned interest. The lady was not a magician after all. It just sounded better if he asked for an advance on his interest.

A reluctant smile tugged at his lips. Not that a paltry euphemism would pass muster with Miss Beddoes. She'd dredge up some quotation and beat him over the head with it. His eyelids began to droop, the book fell from his fingers to the counterpane, and he was asleep.

Chapter Five

HAVERGAL WAS AWAKENED early the next morning by the raucous call of chanticleer. Hearing a rooster, he knew he was in the country, but was unclear for a moment as to precisely where or what he was doing there. Glancing around at the relatively modest and unfamiliar furnishings, he knew he was not at his ancestral home. Then it came back to him, and he emitted a low groan. Miss Beddoes, and Crymont at the inn three miles away with the lightskirts, like a charged pistol waiting to go off. He dragged himself from bed. At least he hadn't overindulged in wine the night before, so his head was clear.

In fact, he found, as he lifted the window and stuck his head out, that he felt remarkably good. It was the early night that had done it. Country smells of meadows, apple blossoms, and the lingering scent of cattle hung on the air. It reminded him of his youth and was a strong contrast to his more recent mornings. He really must change his ways. His conscience had not yet petrified, and he felt badly about his behavior. He inhaled deeply. A country breakfast would hit the spot. He went to the adjoining door and called, "Cuttle."

The unmoving hulk under the blankets told him his valet was still asleep. "Poor masters make poor servants," his father used to say. His conscience gave another jab, as it always did when he thought of his father. Cuttle's services were so seldom required before ten o'clock that he had fallen into the lazy habit of staying abed long after daylight. Havergal advanced and shook him by the toe.

"Gorblimy, it's hardly daylight," Cuttle muttered, but he pushed the blankets aside and got up, grumbling.

Havergal noticed, while Cuttle was assisting him with his toilette, that his valet's eyes were bloodshot and his general air unsteady. "That must have been some drinking spree you had last night?"

"The duke left some wine in the stable."

"That was a pourboire for the servants here at Laurel Hall."

"We shared a few bottles with the house servants. A rare treat it was for them."

"I should think so! That was excellent claret! Bring what's left of it up to my room. We don't want Miss Beddoes accusing us of debasing her servants. And you especially, Cuttle, ought to lay off the drink. It won't do your boxing any good. Look at that paunch! Soft!" he said, touching Cuttle's midriff. His finger sunk into a layer of fat.

"Get me a fight arranged, and I'll get into shape," Cuttle retorted.

The valet had attended to his duties before the drinking bout the night before. His master turned out in a style to do him proud, with Hessians gleaming and cravat immaculate. Havergal appeared a perfect tulip of fashion when he joined the ladies at breakfast half an hour later.

Miss FitzSimmons shot a triumphant glance at Lettie. They had exchanged views as to their guest's probable hour of rising. "Not before noon" was Lettie's opinion.

"I am happy to see you so much recovered," Lettie said when Havergal bowed before them. She was unaware of a smile lifting her lips, but she knew that his appearance gave her pleasure. He looked vitally healthy, so handsome and elegant.

"We thought you might keep later hours," Miss FitzSimmons added with a worried look at Lettie. This was due to the fact that Cook had burned the gammon. They had planned to have a new batch served later.

"I am up with the rooster when in the country." He smiled. He went to the sideboard to help himself to breakfast.

"I'll ask the servants to get some fresh gammon and eggs," Lettie said. "I don't know what ails Cook today. She never burned the gammon before. I hope the stove is not going on us."

"This will be fine," Havergal assured her, and helped himself to some charred meat. The footman who poured his coffee not only slopped the liquid into his saucer, but also made a mess of the table covering.

"I am so dreadfully sorry," Lettie said two or three times. "I really cannot imagine what has come over them. I wonder if they have caught some flu bug. You were feeling poorly last night, Lord Havergal. Did you have any symptoms other than the headache?"

"No, none, and I feel fine today," he assured her.

"Well it is very odd," Miss FitzSimmons said, puzzled. "Let us hope you and I escape it, Lettie, or we shall miss our drive to Canterbury this afternoon."

The afternoon was taken care of in a manner to please the ladies, but there was a long morning in which Havergal hoped to forward his cause by being agreeable. "I hope you have not forgotten your promise to give my grays a try as well, Miss FitzSimmons," he reminded her.

"I look forward to it."

"And you, too, Miss Beddoes," he said, turning to Lettie. Without Norton there to lead the way, he reverted to the proper mode of address.

"The curricle only holds two, does it not?"

"Two at a time. I thought after Miss Fitz-Simmons returns, you might like to try a spin."

"You wanted new gloves for the trip to Canterbury, Lettie," her companion reminded her. "Ashford is only three miles away. You could drive into Ashford with Lord Havergal."

It was the last place Havergal wanted to take her. Ashford meant Crymont, possibly not alone. He never leapt his fences till he came to them, however. By the time they were in the carriage, he could talk her around to some different drive.

"What are you thinking of, Violet?" Lettie said. "Lord Havergal will not want to cool his heels while I go shopping."

"I am an excellent shopper," he offered gallantly. "All the ladies tell me so. My opinion is much sought in the selection of a bonnet or a shawl. Gloves are not my forte, but I know pigskin from kid."

"We shall see." Lettie laughed. She was only human, with the normal feminine weakness of wanting to appear in public with a gallant escort. What a dash she would cut in Ashford! Arriving in Havergal's bang-up curricle, then going on the strut with him. It was more than she could resist. "When do you think you and Miss FitzSimmons will be back?" she asked.

"That depends on when Miss FitzSimmons would like to leave?" he said, turning to Violet and making it a question.

"Is nine o'clock too late?" she asked. "I have a few things to attend to before I go. The chickens are mine," she explained.

He had no notion what care chickens required, but said, "Nine will be fine. It will give me a little time to look over the library and gallery, if Miss Beddoes permits?"

Her smile of relief was perfectly obvious. She found it not so difficult to entertain a viscount as she had feared. With a perfectly inedible breakfast on his plate, Havergal soon rose and asked directions to the library.

"Just down the hall, third door on the left. I'll show you," Lettie said.

The library was the best-furnished room in the house. The Beddoes gentlemen had always been scholars, and the requisite tomes in Latin, Greek, and French had a place on their shelves. The room, too, was lovely. A long wall of windows looked out on the home garden, where flowers were planted next to the house to conceal the rows of cabbages, carrots, onions, and beets beyond. A tall wall of irises stood against the ferny lace of asparagus plants, with sweet peas, lupines, and other modest blooms approaching close to the windows.

"This is charming!" Havergal exclaimed when they entered. He went to the window and looked out a moment, admiring the sun-drenched garden and spreading park beyond the garden.

"It is my favorite room in the house."

After admiring the window view, he turned back to examine the room itself. A pair of long tables ran down the center, with lamps at either end and chairs all around. This seemed a good time to begin flattering her erudition. "Like a dining room for feasting on great works of literature," he said.

There were more comfortable, stuffed chairs in the corners, and a pair drawn up beside the grate.

He strolled toward them. "I wager this is where you and Miss FitzSimmons curl up with a good book on a rainy afternoon." A table between the two chairs held an assortment of magazines, a bonbon dish, and other telltale signs of frequent occupancy. He lifted a book, opened facedown on the table, and glanced at it.

"It is Frances Burney's latest, *The Wanderer*," she said.

"This, I take it, is Miss FitzSimmons's book. What are *you* reading?"

"I am reading that."

"Ah." It was going to be difficult praising her bluestockings if she admitted bluntly to reading Burney. "I rather thought from your conversation yesterday that you were interested in philosophy."

"Oh no. I usually get my philosophy second-hand—that is, I used to, from Papa." She looked rather wistfully at the shelves. "There is a great deal of worthwhile stuff here that I expect I ought to be reading, but somehow when evening comes, I seem too tired to tackle such weighty things."

"If one is truly interested, I expect one would have to set oneself a course and start on it bright and early in the mornings. A sort of university at home." He was willing, indeed eager, to pursue this, with himself as her mentor.

"Yes, I expect so," she said, and revealed her total lack of interest by turning away. "I shall leave you to the books. The gallery is just across the hall. I will be happy to accompany you when you are ready. Our pictures, I fear, were not executed by artists you will immediately recognize, but are mostly family portraits by local painters. Unlike books, the works of the best painters are not so easily available." She smiled and turned to leave.

Havergal felt he was getting along famously with Miss Beddoes and wanted to continue the conversation. "Wait! Let us go to the gallery now—if you are at leisure, that is," he said, fearful that he was imposing.

"Yes, certainly."

The gallery was not what Havergal would call a gallery. It was just a large rectangular room with portraits down either side and sofas and tables at either end. "This is Josiah Beddoes, the man who built Laurel Hall in 1695," she said at the first portrait. A glowering visage with piercing eyes glared at them. "Josiah was an officer. He went to Ireland with William the Third and was rewarded with land here when they won the Battle of the Boyne."

"Ah, a military family."

"Just so, and this is Josiah's son, Thomas. He was at the siege of Gibraltar. He was the last soldier. As the family seemed to produce only one male in each generation, they gave up soldiering and went to court. Till my grandfather's time, that is. He had no use for London and turned into a country squire."

They continued down the wall, looking at the pictures of ancestral squires and their wives. Havergal scraped his mind clean to conjure up compliments. By the time they got to Lettie's father, he had run dry, so he turned to her favorite topic, young Tom. "Soon your brother must have his portrait taken," he said.

"Not for a few years yet. He will wait till he has reached full manhood. He is only one and twenty."

"He would be offended to hear you say he is not a man at one and twenty."

"Men mature more slowly than women, I think" is all she said, but he soon read a slur into it.

"I hope you will remember to have him call on me when he goes up to London. I will be happy to help see him settled."

"That is very kind of you."

They were finished with the tour, and while Havergal felt they were on a slightly firmer footing, he wished to advance further. With a lady no course occurred to him except flirtation. "Is it not the custom for the young ladies of the house to have their likenesses taken?" he asked. "I don't mean to deride your ancestors, but a few more pictures of ladies would improve your collection a hundredfold. If the daughters were all so pretty as yourself, Miss Beddoes . . ." He gave a charming smile.

Lettie had virtually no experience in flirting, and none with such an accomplished flirt as Lord Havergal. She felt woefully out of her depth and stiffened in embarrassment. "It is the custom for ladies to have their pictures hung in their husbands' galleries, I believe. If I marry, then I shall be painted."

"If?" he exclaimed, feigning astonishment. "Surely you mean *when*, Miss Beddoes. The gents must be lined up for miles. I am surprised you have waited so long to accept—that is—not that I mean to imply you are—" He came to a stumbling halt. *Dolt!*

"I am seven and twenty, like you, Lord Havergal. Three months older, actually."

"Is that all?" The horrible words were out, echoing endlessly in the still room, while Havergal stood, openmouthed at his own incredible gaucherie, and Miss Beddoes stared dumbly, as if she had been struck. "Not that I mean twenty-seven is old! Good gracious, I consider myself quite a young sprout, I promise you." He laughed inanely to cover his gêne.

As his full meaning sunk in, Lettie felt as if she had been bludgeoned with a hammer. Bad enough to be seven and twenty and single, but to hear from a gentleman that he took her for much older was a severe blow. "Yes, appearances to the contrary, that is all," she said in a glacial tone. "A female of seven and twenty years is called a spinster, not a sprout," she added, reigning in the urge to crown him.

He saw her jaws working in vexation, saw a moist sparkle in her eyes, and was seized with a dreadful premonition that she was going to cry. His warm sympathy was engaged at once, and he reached for her hands. "I'm sorry, Miss Beddoes. I ought to be drawn and quartered for that. It is this bizarre business of your being my guardian. I came expecting an old man, and having got over the shock of your being a woman—*lady*—I am still grappling with the fact that you are young."

She whipped her hands away, fighting back tears of anger and shame. "You must not feel compelled to sympathize, Lord Havergal. I am not quite on the verge of expiring yet. I doubt you will expect condolences in three months when you reach my advanced years. Though of course you will not have to face the odium of being called a spinster," she added tartly.

"What's in a name?" he asked, trying to lighten the mood. "I see you have not put on your caps in any case." He let his eyes linger admiringly on her black hair. It formed an attractive frame around her pale face, coming to a point in the middle of her forehead. He found himself gazing into her eyes. She had truly fine eyes, her best feature. Serious eyes, dark gray with golden flecks.

Lettie was flustered at that look and spoke brusquely to hide her embarrassment. "I did, two years ago, but I took them off again."

"Ah—you met a gentleman!" he said roguishly.

"I found the caps a nuisance. They kept slipping off. Would you like to go back to the library now? Perhaps some coffee and a fire . . ."

"Please, don't trouble yourself. I have just had coffee, and it is warm enough to do without a fire.

In fact, I believe I'll just step out into that charming garden."

"If you like."

"Are you the gardener?"

"I have an herb garden. Violet does the flowers."

"That is appropriate!" he exclaimed. She gave him a blank look. "Violet—flowers," he said, feeling foolish.

"Oh, yes. And I expect that makes me an herb."

"No, an herbalist," he said, defeated. Some men, Samuel Johnson decreed, were not clubbable. Miss Beddoes was not flirtable.

He left, feeling as foolish as he had ever felt in his life. What a thing to say! God, quite apart from wanting to get Miss Beddoes into a good mood, that was a wretched thing to say to any older lady. And she looked so stricken. She wasn't really *that* old. He would be especially nice to her during the rest of the day.

Lettie remained behind, thinking. The meeting and Havergal's awkward outburst had devastated her. To make the matter worse, she had taken the ridiculous idea that he wanted her company when he asked her to show him the gallery. Wanted it not just to plead for his money, but to be with her. In short, she thought he found her attractive, and all along he thought she was an old lady. He *pitied* her. She saw the sympathy in his eyes when he reached for her fingers. He was an impulsive creature. Quick to wound by a thoughtless word and quick to regret it. A man ruled by his passions. She had never met one before.

And it was his passion for gambling that brought him here, that forced him to be civil to her. She knew it perfectly well. Yet even knowing it, knowing he thought her an old lady, she could not totally harden her heart against him. The way he had studied her hair and face when they were talking about caps—the admiration in his eyes had seemed genuine, and he hadn't mentioned the money again. In any case, she would enjoy the trip into Ashford on his arm. How her friends would stare!

She went upstairs to look over her bonnets and select the most attractive for the outing. She had bought a new bonnet for springtime, but it would not do in the open carriage. Standing in front of her mirror, she frowned at her coiffure, her face, and her gown. Plain, countrified. She was not only old, but an old dowdy. She wished with all her heart she had some dashing London gowns to put on and astonish Havergal, but she had no such articles. She turned from the mirror and left the room.

She glanced in an open door to a guest room as she went down the hall. To her utter astonishment, she saw Jamie, a lower footman, sitting on the bed with his head in his hands. She hurried in. "Jamie, what is the matter?" she asked.

He lifted a pale face and looked at her with bloodshot eyes. "I think I'm coming down with something, mum," he said weakly.

"Oh dear! And Cook was feeling poorly, too. I must have Dr. Cooley in. You'd best go to bed. It is fortunate we are dining out this evening, for it seems the whole household of servants has taken ill."

Her greater concern was that she would take ill herself to cause further ravages to her appearance, with the treat of a curricle ride and the trip to Canterbury awaiting her. She sent for the doctor and went to her room. Through the window she saw Havergal strolling through the garden. He seemed genuinely interested in it. Odd, to see a city buck like Havergal enjoying a country garden. How attractive he looked, even from this height. A squirrel caught his attention, and he made a game of trying to draw it nearer. It ignored him. He leaned forward and smelled the honeysuckle, then snapped off a twig and stuck it in his lapel. When he took the path to the stable, she left the window.

The face in the mirror reassured her that she wasn't ill. She looked a little more tired than usual, but it was Havergal's infamous comment that accounted for that. His presence in the house and the duke's pending visit lent an unusual excitement to her day and prevented further repining. What was there to regret? She was only a few minutes older than when she had gone into the gallery, and she felt fine then. She was twenty-seven, not ninety-seven. What difference did age make anyway? You were only as old as you felt, and on this spring day she felt young. Havergal and his opinions were nothing to her.

The sunshine and flowers beyond her window lifted her heart. It was spring, and there was the assembly looming close. She felt, for the first time in years, a young restlessness and a determination to wrest a few surprises from life before she really was old. Havergal hadn't thought twenty-seven too old for marriage in any case.

She lifted her new spring bonnet from its form and examined it. She must keep it for Canterbury, but she put it on and examined herself. It was a more dashing bonnet than she usually wore, and the strange thing was that Violet had accused her of buying a widow's bonnet when she came home with it. The plain black straw had been rather severe, so she added a ribbon and a flower. A narrow band of pink satin encircled the crown, and from the brim one pink rose peeped flirtatiously. It was not a deb's bonnet, but a bonnet for a dashing older lady. Her only fear was that it was too sophisticated for Ashford, but it was certainly not too sophisticated for a duke and a viscount—and an archbishop.

Chapter Six

Lᴇᴛᴛɪᴇ ꜰɪʟʟᴇᴅ ᴛʜᴇ time till Violet and Havergal returned from their outing by arranging tomorrow's dinner party. This meant a battle with Mrs. Siddons to augment the already lavish meal, but first she studied her guest list, seeing it with her new guests' eyes. Mr. Norton was the last person she wanted to have sit down with the duke and Lord Havergal, but he was a close friend, and he would be mortally wounded if he were put off. No, unthinkable to offend her friends to impress mere acquaintances. And there was Miss Millie, Norton's sister cum housekeeper. The Smallbones from the next estate were presentable, and that left only the vicar and his wife to round it off. No apologies were required for a vicar, but her mind *would* compare him to the Archbishop of Canterbury. That made a total of five couples, ten people in all, about as ill-sorted a group as she had ever assembled under her roof.

At least it was only for dinner. They would be leaving immediately after for the assembly. She called Cook into her office for the confrontation regarding the new menu.

"I don't suppose turtle soup is possible?" Lettie asked doubtfully.

Cook rustled her aprons and sniffed. "Where would we be getting a turtle, mum? There's never been a turtle in Ashford."

"Fish then. A nice fresh salmon."

"The fishmonger likes a week's warning for salmon. I've ordered turbot, which will do as well with my white sauce." Lettie gave up pretending she had anything to say about the menu, and Cook continued. "Luckily I have a brace of dandy green geese hanging out back. With some of our own mutton, peas, and turnips you need not blush for your dinner."

"And pork for Mr. Norton. Now for dessert, perhaps that peach cake with cream?"

"We ate the last of the peach preserves when your uncle was here last week."

"Pity."

"I can substitute apples."

"Oh not *apples*, Cook. I want something *special*."

"I'll have a look at my book and come up with something grand enough for a duke's tooth, never fear."

"Make sure you don't burn it. The gammon at breakfast was wretched." Cook gave a mutinous look. "I expect you have a touch of whatever is ailing all the servants," Lettie said forgivingly. "You do look a little flushed, Mrs. Siddons."

Her cook made no reply to this but just rose silently and left, feeling as guilty as sin. It was that half bottle Cuttle had left behind the night before that had done the mischief. Siddons was dead set against her drinking. She only meant to taste it, but it was so good, and she was hot and tired from making her bread. At least the mistress was in the dark about it—and Siddons would never give her away.

At ten o'clock Miss FitzSimmons arrived home, her bonnet askew, her hair flying out from under it, her cheeks pink, and her smile as broad as the sofa.

"It is incredible, Lettie. Sixteen miles an hour! I felt I was *flying*. We passed Mr. Smallbone and nearly bowled him off the road, but Havergal is such an excellent fiddler that he squeaked us past unharmed. Bundle up, for the wind nearly carries you away."

"Good gracious, Violet! You're all blown to pieces."

"So exhilarating! There is nothing like it. Havergal is waiting out front."

"Havergal? You sound very familiar."

"He asked me to stop calling him Lord Havergal. And he called me Violet," she confessed. It was hard to tell, but Lettie thought she was blushing—and well she might.

"I am surprised at you, Violet. No, I am *more* than surprised. I am shocked. You have known Mr. Norton ten years and have never called him Ned. You scarcely know Lord Havergal."

"London manners," Violet said offhandedly. "We do not wish to appear too provincial."

"What is truly provincial is a belief that London is the top of the world—and an eagerness to ape London manners," she added tartly.

Yet as Lettie lifted her plain round bonnet to put on, she wished it were a smarter, more London-looking bonnet. She tied the ribbons tightly under her chin and went out. This was her first view of Havergal's dashing curricle. It gleamed golden yellow in the sun, accoutred with much gleaming silver. The frisky grays harnessed up to it appeared perfectly fresh. They pawed the ground in their eagerness to be off. It occurred to Lettie that the seat was very high off the ground and very insecurely guarded. A railing only eight inches high was all that held the passenger in her seat. Even getting into that high seat promised some difficulty.

Havergal leapt down from his perch and came to her assistance. The marauding wind that had undone Violet's coiffure left Havergal's untouched. No wisps of hair escaped the curled beaver, set at a jaunty angle on his head. His face was ruddy, but his complexion was customarily high.

"It's not as treacherous as it looks," he smiled, seeing her consternation. "Just put one foot here," he continued, indicating a metal disk that served as a toehold.

He steadied her with an arm around her waist as she ascended. It was not a flirtatious gesture. No unnecessary pressure was applied, nor did the hand linger, but Lettie was aware of the latent strength in the arm that protected her. When she was safely ensconced, Havergal lifted his head and smiled. She felt a tug of attraction toward that winning smile.

"It's quite comfortable really," she admitted.

He vaulted up to the seat beside her and took the reins. "You sound surprised, Miss Beddoes. Did you think I would submit you to any danger?"

"Not purposely," she allowed.

He gave the team the office to be off. Lettie's neck jerked back at the unexpected speed of their take-off. As the team continued at a fast, though steady, pace through the park toward the main road, she settled down to a rather nervous enjoyment of the sensation. Riding in an open curricle was a completely different sensation from rattling along at seven or eight miles an hour in her own lumbering carriage. The sun seemed brighter, the scenery greener, and the whole experience much more exciting. She felt like a goddess, sitting high on her throne, looking down on mere mortals below.

They were fast approaching the main road, and

Havergal wanted to steer her away from Ashford. He was by no means certain Crymont would have sent the girls home yet. They had come from London to Ashford yesterday. Certainly they had remained overnight, and if they left without touring the shops, it was more than he dared to count on.

"I took Miss FitzSimmons to Kingsnorth," he said. "Shall we go that way? The drive is pretty."

"You forget, Lord Havergal. You were to take me to Ashford to purchase new gloves."

Her reply left little room for maneuvering. His heart sank. "There was a very pretty shop at Kingsnorth."

"Not so good as Mercer's, in Ashford. I have seen the gloves I want to buy. I shan't keep you dawdling about the rows of buttons and pins for an hour, if that is what you fear," she replied, still in good humor.

He risked one more putting-off sally. "Why don't we drive west, toward Tonbridge? I've never been that way."

"There is virtually nothing on that road till you reach Tonbridge," she pointed out.

"Let us go to Tonbridge."

"When we are driving all the way to Canterbury this afternoon? You are fond of driving, Lord Havergal. Much fonder than I. Ashford will be far enough. You turn right here," she said as they reached the main road.

He had no choice but to do as she asked. He did not give up entirely, however. It was still three miles to Ashford. He would discover some diversion along the way. At every byway he slowed down and inquired what lay down that road.

"Only Norton's farm," she replied the first time. Another time it was "The local abattoir. I cannot believe you would want to go there." When he inquired a third time, Lettie found it strange. "Do

66

you have some particular aversion to being seen with me in Ashford, sir?" she asked quite briskly.

Her interpretation of his reluctance threw him off balance. "I don't know what you mean," he said in confusion. "What aversion could I possibly have to being seen in your company?"

"I don't know either, unless it is this horrid bonnet, for my character is excellent, I promise you." She carefully avoided any mention of her advanced years.

"Better than mine, certainly," he returned with a teasing smile. "It is *your* reputation I fear for, you see, being seen on the strut with that wastrel, Havergal. That is what my friends call me, Havergal. I wish you would do the same." He lifted his blue eyes and examined her fleetingly. "And the bonnet, by the by, is charming."

After that bit of innocent flirtation, Lettie was much inclined to do as he suggested and dispense with the "Lord," but as she had delivered Violet a lecture, she felt some demur was necessary. "We are hardly more than acquaintances," she pointed out.

"We are connections through Horace's marriage to your—what was she—cousin?"

"Yes, but—"

"And you are my guardian. Now surely a charge may call his guardian by her Christian name when he is shamelessly battening himself on her. You cannot call on propriety, Miss Beddoes. We have been carrying on a most improper, clandestine correspondence for a twelvemonth. It is high time we stop *lord*ing and *miss*ing each other. I shan't 'miss' you till I leave," he joked. "That is a pun, ma'am. Are you not going to remind me of Dennis's excellent set-down: 'A man who could make so vile a pun would not hesitate to pick a man's pocket.' Come now, show me your claws."

"By deriding your own conversation, you leave me nothing to say."

He turned a jeering smile in her direction. "You could say I might call you Lettie."

"Very well then. You may call me Lettie," she said primly.

He acknowledged it with a gallant bow and a smile. His eyes soon veered left to another road and another possibility of reprieve. "Don't even think it," she said. "An extremely bizarre hermit lives in a cave down that road. He shoots anyone who trespasses."

"I don't see any signs posted."

"You'll feel the bullets if you dare to enter."

To offer any further objections to Ashford would only confirm her suspicions, so Havergal steeled himself for the visit. He'd whisk her in and out of the shop as quickly as possible and pray they didn't meet Crymont and his friends.

"You can stable your rig at the Royal Oak," she mentioned when they entered the town.

His heart sank to his boots. "I'll just leave it at the curb."

"We might bump into Crymont at the inn," she tempted.

He controlled his shiver and replied, "You said you would not be long."

"I thought you might like to stroll down High Street. There is a church with a rather fine perpendicular tower toward the end of the street. It has some interesting monuments and brasses. Or perhaps you are not interested in churches?"

"One cathedral a day is usually enough for me," he said, reminding her of the trip to Canterbury.

Canterbury was not Ashford. No one she knew would see her with Havergal there. She sighed and pointed out the drapery shop a block away.

Havergal scanned the street. It was not so very

busy at an early hour in the morning. He saw at a glance that Crymont was not about and decided to risk the stroll to please her, but he dare not stable his rig at the Royal Oak. He tossed a street urchin a coin to hold his team while they entered the shop. The purchase of the gloves took only minutes, as she had promised. What took so much time was being presented to her friends. Miss Beddoes seemed to know every soul in the shop, presented them all to him, and did it with a peculiarly proprietary air.

Havergal was not a vain man, but it eventually occurred to him that she was showing off her exhibit. She wanted her friends to see she had a young lord, a bachelor, staying with her. It was her friends who slyly inquired for Lady Havergal, and Miss Beddoes was not slow to enlighten them of his marital status. Some corner of her cast-iron mind had taken note of the fact that he was eligible, then. Perhaps she was not so unflirtable as he thought.

When he had done the pretty with half a dozen ladies, they went back outside. A quick perusal of the street told him Crymont was still not about. He allowed himself to be taken to admire the church. Knowing Crymont would never venture inside a church, he felt safe to linger there, admiring the tombs and brasses. After a lengthy perusal, it was Lettie who suggested they should leave.

"For we have to drive home, have lunch, change, and get to Canterbury. Pretty hard trotting for one day."

Havergal laughed, taking it for a joke. "And that still leaves us the evening," he said. "You are forgetting the duke is taking us to dinner."

"Forget it?" she asked in astonishment. "No indeed, that is the best part! I was just going over the day's activities."

"Dinner with a duke is better than visiting an

archbishop? I am shocked, Lettie. Your morality is slipping," he said, and laughed—right in church.

It was an infectious laugh. Or perhaps it was the busy rush of new and unusual activities that lent a special charm to that morning. Or even his using her first name so casually, as if they were old friends. "Shocking, is it not?" she agreed. "But I have met a few archbishops before. Crymont is my first duke."

He took her arm and escorted her back to the curricle. "We lesser peers, of course, are not worth mentioning," he said with an expression of mock abuse. "No, it is not necessary to apologize, Lettie. You would not be in alt to meet a vicar or curate, and you are not impressed to be dining with a viscount—and a poor wasted viscount with his pockets to let besides."

"Quite so, especially when said viscount is only here with a view to conning me into padding out those pockets."

Lettie was at ease with the curricle now. She put her foot on the mounting disc and felt less strange when Havergal put his arm around her.

"Conning? That is a hard word, ma'am. It suggests deceit. Begging is more like it."

"Come now, Havergal. Admit you want the blunt to pay off your gambling debts."

"Will it change your mind?"

"Certainly. My opinion of you would be better if you at least told the truth."

"But would you forward me the money?"

"No."

"So much for that then. I want to improve my hunting box. I *do* want to, you know, so it is not precisely a lie. It is just that I don't plan to do so at this time, with this money."

"That is the merest sophistry, sir. You misled me."

He gave her a resigned look and shook his head. "No, I only tried to. You're too clever by half, *Mr.* Beddoes. As I have confessed my misdemeanor, won't you admit you led me astray there on purpose?"

"I will allow that I let you lead yourself astray."

"Why?" he asked, truly curious.

"I feared you might dislike having a lady control you."

"That is nothing new for me," he replied with a quizzing laugh. "How's the gout, L.A.?" he asked, and jiggled the reins for the horses to take off. Accustomed to the suddeness of their start, Lettie prepared herself and saved her neck a rude jolt.

When he had set a steady pace, Lettie pursued the topic. "The thing is, Havergal, I cannot forward you the thousand without eating into your capital, and I promised Horace I would not do that. That is precisely why he appointed me, to protect the money for you. There is not yet a thousand pounds of interest accrued, you see," she said, as though explaining it to an imbecile.

"I know," he said hastily. "I do have *some* acquaintance with money management, you know."

"Yes, a fleeting acquaintance, but a gentleman in your position ought to be well and thoroughly grounded. You will have all your father's money and estates to manage one day. It would be criminal to run through them as you do through lesser sums."

His anger spewed up, but he knew she was right, and that she would hound him till he admitted it. "You're right. I know it perfectly well in my *head*, but in my *heart*, I keep thinking money is to spend and enjoy."

"One can do that, too, if he does it wisely. Is there no way you can retrench? I know your father gives you what seems to me a splendid allowance."

71

"Certainly I could—and shall. In fact, I made a firm resolution last night to reform, but gambling debts cannot wait on good intentions. They must be paid promptly."

"Is there anything you can sell?"

"I have my team up for auction at Tatt's."

Lettie looked ruefully at the proud heads and heaving flanks of the team. "That is a pity, for I know they are great favorites of yours, but perhaps it is a good lesson. Losing your team may drive home how profligate you have become."

"Not this team, actually. It is a spare set of carriage horses I spoke of."

"I see. Then my pity is misplaced. Sell them," she said firmly, "and in the future try if you can to live within your means."

Havergal was within a heartbeat of delivering Miss Beddoes a lecture of his own. It was unbearable to have to listen to these platitudes from a provincial miss no wiser and not that much older than himself. While the words were forming into coherence, he glanced down the road and saw Cherry Devereau's landau fast approaching. Everything else fell from his mind as catastrophe came bolting toward him.

The carriage top was down to let them enjoy the fine spring weather. Cherry, Iona, and Crymont sat in full view. The ladies wore high-poke bonnets garnished with a quantity of flowers and ribbons not worn by ladies of the *ton*. It was Havergal's intention to bolt past without stopping, but in his agitation he pulled on the reins, and his team slowed.

Miss Devereau's driver, recognizing Lord Havergal's curricle, likewise drew on the reins. The carriages pulled alongside each other and stopped. It would be difficult to say who was more surprised, Havergal or Crymont, who thought his friend must

72

have run mad, stopping for a chat with a pair of lightskirts when he was with Miss Beddoes.

Crymont lifted his curled beaver and bowed his head. "Miss Beddoes. A lovely day," he said.

"It is lovely. Are you taking your friends to see the church?" she asked. While she spoke, Lettie's smile was turned equally on the duke and his companions. Unaccustomed to the niceties of London fashion, she knew only that she was looking at two of the most beautiful and fashionable females she had ever seen. Their toilette was a trifle brighter and more highly garnished than she would wear herself, but then the ladies were young. Probably noble connections or friends of Crymont.

"Church? Oh I shouldn't think so. Just a drive."

"Well, don't be late. Remember, we are to leave for Canterbury at two-thirty." She looked expectantly, waiting for Crymont to present his friends to her. The ladies, she noticed, were giving her sharp looks.

"Quite. Quite."

Lettie was hard put to account for his embarrassment and looked to Havergal for the introduction. He was glaring at the duke with a face made of stone. "Good day, Crymont. Ladies," he said, and urged his team on.

Lettie looked over her shoulder and waved. The ladies gave a desultory wave in reply. Crymont bowed.

"That is odd," she said. "Why did he not introduce us?"

Havergal couldn't believe she didn't realize the girls' profession and was, of course, eager to keep her in the dark. "I've no idea."

"Do you know them?"

"The blonde looked familiar. A Miss Devereau, I believe."

"She is very pretty. Beautiful, really."

"Yes, she's attractive."

"Why did *you* not introduce me? Were you ashamed to be seen with such a country mouse in front of your fine friends, Havergal?" she asked with a bold smile, though she wondered if she had hit on the truth.

"Don't be ridiculous," he scowled.

"I sense some deep mystery here. Pray tell me what it is. Are Miss Devereau and the duke meeting clandestinely?"

He leapt on this idea. "I expect that's it. His family would never favor the match."

"Is there something amiss with Miss Devereau? Perhaps she is poor—though she doesn't look it. Such a handsome landau."

"Undowered ladies often try to keep up a particularly good appearance to fool the unwary bachelors."

"I shall tease the truth out of the duke this afternoon," she said, and settled back comfortably to enjoy the drive home.

The newly leafed trees formed a canopy overhead, and sunlight dappled the roadway. The sky was a brilliant blue with hardly a cloud in sight. It was a lovely day, and now a mystery and a romance to make it complete. A whole day and evening of unaccustomed liveliness sparkled enticingly before her. It didn't seem that life could offer more. Her sole regret was that life had waited so long to favor her.

Havergal, relieved at having escaped catastrophe, forgave Lettie for her lecture and put himself out to be entertaining. The drive passed all too quickly for her. When she described her morning to Miss FitzSimmons later, she called their guest Havergal, as easily as though she had never called him anything else.

Violet lifted her eyes to the ceiling and said

softly, "If I were ten years younger, I would toss my bonnet at him."

"So would I," Lettie answered unthinkingly.

"Why Lettie, you are only a few months older. That is not to be taken into account."

"What is to be taken into account is that I am an ancient spinster of twenty-seven years, whereas he is a young sprout of the same age. Yet there is a difference of about a decade in there somewhere. All the noble debs in London must be after him. The ladies I saw with the duke this morning were gorgeous. Besides, his character is shockingly unstable," she added, though in less accusatory accents than before.

"Yes, but in a strange way, I find that a part of his charm. Never quite knowing if he is going to be a trifle indiscreet. I'm sure he means no harm."

"That is true." She knew at least that he had regretted his outburst about her age. "He meant no harm."

Chapter Seven

THE DRIVE TO Canterbury proved a letdown. It was
not only that the archbishop was in London, though
that was a hard blow for Miss FitzSimmons. For
Lettie, the greater disappointment was the abra-
sive nature of the afternoon's conversation. She had
been anticipating a delightful drive with two handsome and eligible peers, and instead found herself
acting as referee between a pair of squabbling
young men.

The drive began auspiciously enough. Crymont
expressed himself delighted at her new bonnet.
Havergal, too, she thought, liked it. He did not add
his compliments to the lavish surfeit of Crymont's,
but he smiled and lifted his eyebrows in an approving way that pleased her.

The pleasantries broke down as soon as they were
on their way, and Lettie said, "Why did you not
present me to your friends this morning, Duke?
They looked charming."

She noticed that Havergal glared at him as before, and the duke stared back questioningly. "I expect Havergal has told you something on that
score," he said vaguely.

"Only an enticing hint that the meeting was clandestine."

"Exactly," the duke said. "It was a clandestine meeting, which is why I could not introduce you."

"You cannot think I would have told anyone! I don't know Miss Devereau."

"He told you it was Miss Devereau!" the duke exclaimed, staring at Havergal. It was inconceivable to him that Miss Devereau's scarlet eminence was not known, even in Ashford. She had knocked Harriet Wilson, the reigning courtesan, right off the map in London.

"Your secret is safe with me. I don't know any of her family, or yours," Lettie pointed out.

"Miss Devereau doesn't have any family," the duke said austerely.

"I see. Well, she is very beautiful in any case."

"Her friend is also very pretty, even if *some people* choose to reject her," the duke replied with another of those scathing looks to Havergal.

"What is her friend's name?" Miss FitzSimmons asked him.

"Miss Hardy. Iona Hardy."

"Are the girls related?"

"Friends. Just friends. Miss Devereau has no family," he repeated.

"You must feel free to bring them to call on us if they are still in town tomorrow, Duke," Violet said.

Lettie noticed the duke shoot a triumphant glance to Havergal at Miss FitzSimmons's invitation and wondered at it. Havergal seemed determined to keep her from meeting those ladies.

"The girls have left, have they not, Crymont?" Havergal said in a strangely commanding accent.

"They have decided to remain another day." Crymont wore an air of victory, and Havergal was fairly steaming at this news. "But I doubt they will be up to a visit. Miss Hardy is feeling poorly," Crymont added.

The conversation veered to other subjects, but the cheerful mood of the morning was never recaptured. A closed carriage, even such a well-sprung and extravagantly upholstered one as the duke's, was no match for the open curricle, though the knowledge that strawberry leaves decorated the door did much to raise its value once they entered Canterbury. They had all seen the cathedral, and when it transpired that the archbishop was away, they did no more than take a quick run through it.

Next came a stroll along the Stour River to admire the watered meadows and have Lettie explain the hop gardens to Crymont. Before leaving, they took some refreshment at the Rose in High Street. It occurred to Lettie that if the poor spirits of the afternoon continued into the evening, the dinner party would be as flat as this outing.

"Perhaps we shall meet your friends at the hotel this evening at dinner," she said hopefully. Silence descended like a pall over the table.

"Shall I invite them, Havergal?" the duke asked mischievously.

"Do as you think best," Havergal replied with an air of indifference, and quickly finished his wine.

After the ladies had been delivered home and Havergal remained a minute chatting to the duke at the carriage, Lettie and Violet retired to the latter's bedchamber to discuss the outing. "There is some mystery about those ladies, I know it," Lettie said.

"I sensed the hostility every time they were mentioned. Very likely the lads are both in love with one of them."

Lettie gave a gasp of surprise. "That's it!" she exclaimed. "It would be the blonde, Miss Devereau. I don't think Havergal even knew Miss Hardy, though the duke was hinting him in her direction. Havergal is in love with Miss Devereau, and the duke is cutting him out. It is just as well, too, for she has no dowry. Havergal ought to marry a wealthy lady, unless he puts it off till he inherits his father's estate. But it is odd Havergal didn't want them joining us for dinner, is it not?"

"No doubt she is tempted by Crymont's superior title and wealth. He would prefer to have her to himself."

"So much for my tossing my bonnet at him," Lettie said, and gave a resigned shrug.

"It is all conjecture. We may be far off the mark. Perhaps Havergal owes Miss Devereau money. That would account for his stiffness every time you mention her."

"I cannot think he would borrow from a lady, Violet. Surely he is not *that* shabby."

They were interrupted by a servant telling them that Mr. Norton had called during their absence. She handed Lettie a note, in which he requested the honor of calling on her and Miss FitzSimmons that evening. He usually came without permission, but he knew Lettie had company and was trying out noble manners.

"I must answer this at once. I daresay his nose will be out of joint when I refuse."

"Yes, and a bit of jealousy might bring him to the sticking point," Violet replied, not entirely happy with the possibility.

"Oh Lord, I hope he does not start *that* again."

At Crymont's carriage, it was the duke's behavior that was under attack. "Why didn't you send them packing?" Havergal demanded. "Get rid of them, at once! Disaster was only avoided by a hair this morning when we met. And tonight they'll be at the inn while we're dining belowstairs."

"They refused to leave. You know Cherry has a mind of her own. And Iona was in the boughs, the way you've been ignoring her after she came pelting all the way to Ashford."

"I don't even *know* her! This is all *your* doing."

"I did it for you, Havergal. Iona is very eager to meet you."

"Well I am not eager to meet her. What would Miss Beddoes think if she realized?"

"Are you making headway with the Terrible Turk, then?"

"Not really," he admitted. "The woman's an oak, Crymont. She won't bend an inch."

"Then we might as well leave tomorrow. And it won't matter if she *does* find out, will it?"

"We can't leave. We've promised to escort the ladies to the assembly."

"They'll find other escorts or go by themselves."

Havergal frowned at the duke's selfishness. "It means something to them to have a pair of noble gents squire them to the party, Crymont. I can tell by the way Lettie was showing me off this morning. I cannot like to disappoint her."

"It might be amusing to watch the provincials fawn on us," Crymont said thoughtfully. "I have noticed the London debs aren't so warm this year. Their mamas are warning them off from us, I expect."

"We are hardly that bad!" Havergal exclaimed, shocked. Certainly *he* had noticed no diminution of attention.

"My reputation has had a few more years' battering than yours, of course. In three years you, too, will be squinted at with suspicion."

Havergal listened and reminded himself again of the necessary reformation. "I would not want Lettie to think me a womanizer as well as a gambling fool."

Crymont examined his friend through narrowed eyes. "This is a new twist, my friend. She can't keep your interest from you or the whole capital when you are thirty. If she won't give you the advance, there's no need to worry for your reputation in that quarter."

But he *was* worried. Common sense could not account for it. Her control was limited, and the likelihood of her caving in was minimal, yet he wanted her good opinion nearly as much as he wanted to conceal it from Crymont. After long years of reckless living, he was embarrassed to confess that he still maintained a shred of character and a lingering desire for redemption.

"Unless you have developed a *tendre* for Miss Beddoes?" Crymont said sardonically. "I always liked those tall Tartars myself, but she ain't in your preferred style."

"She knows my papa," he said, unhappy with this prevarication.

"Ah. She could serve you well there, then. That explains it. But about Iona—the girls are becoming restive, Havergal. I promised them we would entertain them this evening. Give them a late supper—after we deliver Miss Beddoes and her companion home, I mean. I fear if you don't go along with it, they'll do something rash—like joining our dinner party. . . ."

Havergal didn't know much about Iona Hardy, but he knew Cherry Devereau would stop at very little. Her success had gone to her lovely head. She behaved with wanton abandon and a total disregard for propriety. To ensure a peaceful dinner, he agreed to go back to the inn after delivering the ladies home to Laurel Hall.

During the next hour, Lettie wrote her reply to Mr. Norton and made her toilette. At six she and Violet sat in state in the saloon, awaiting Havergal's descent. Lettie drew in her breath sharply when he appeared in his black pantaloons and well-fitting black jacket, with a gleam of white shirt to set it off. He was a perfect gothic hero come to life in her saloon.

"I have ordered your carriage, as your curricle would not hold the three of us," Lettie mentioned.

"I might have known I could count on your fore-thought," Havergal replied.

She felt a swell of pleasure at the spontaneous compliment. It sounded more sincere than the following string of praise on her and Violet's toilettes. She was coming to know him well enough to tell when he meant what he was saying or was merely trying to flatter her. They left immediately and were soon at the Royal Oak.

The duke met them at the doorway and ushered them personally to his private parlor, where an elaborate table was laid. "You look even lovelier than I have been anticipating," he said, lifting Lettie's hand to his lips.

She hardly knew how to reply to such high praise and said, "Thank you, sir," in a stilted way.

"I have brought my own wine with me," he continued, handing the ladies a glass of excellent champagne. "I always travel with my own wine and my own linen."

"What, you carry sheets and pillowcases around with you?" Miss FitzSimmons asked, shocked at such extravagance. "I am surprised you don't travel with your own company, in case you find nothing at the inn to suit you."

"What a clever idea!" the duke answered with a sly look at Havergal.

"I had hoped we might meet Miss Devereau and her friend," Lettie said, throwing Havergal into a spasm of alarm.

"Unfortunately the ladies had to return to London," the duke said, "but I trust we shall be merry without them."

"I'm sure we shall. And in any case, it would have been a sad blow to the local ladies if they had come to our assembly and stolen all the gentlemen from us."

"Never from you, I am sure, Miss Beddoes," he said with another bow.

"I was never a match for Miss Devereau, even in my youth. At my age I certainly cannot lay claim to be an Incomparable," she said frankly.

"That claim must come from the opposite sex, and I hereby proclaim you an Incomparable, Miss Beddoes," the duke said.

She gave him a saucy smile. "And I, sir, proclaim you a flatterer."

"Havergal will tell you I never flatter any lady under thirty. Above thirty, flattery is not only permissible but de rigueur. That was tactless," he said, turning to Miss FitzSimmons, "for I judge you to be nearing thirty, madam."

This sophistry was received with a blushing smile by Miss FitzSimmons. The evening was off to a fine start. Champagne flowed freely, and the meal provided was excellent. When His Grace entreated Miss Beddoes to send her brother to him upon his arrival in London, the last of Lettie's coolness evaporated. The duke was allowed to be unexceptionable.

"I have two pocket boroughs in my control," he explained. "If Tom wishes to stand for Parliament, the thing is done. If, on the other hand, he is interested in an appointed position, my godfather, Bathurst, will find him a spot. Or any of the Cabinet. I am connected to most of them."

"Your offer quite puts mine in the shade," Havergal said dampingly. "I have offered to help Tom find a spot, Crymont."

"Ah, I am stepping on some toes here, I perceive. We shall both be active on his behalf. Havergal among the Whigs, and I among the Tories. Take care or you will find your brother Lord Mayor of London, Miss Beddoes." A shadow of a smile moved his lips.

"I was beginning to have visions of his being prime minister," Lettie returned with a broader smile.

"But then he would be required to live on Downing Street, and he would not be comfortable there, I promise you. A damp, crowded little domicile. I see him in a mansion in Berkeley Square."

"You are too ridiculous!" Lettie laughed. "But I do thank you for your kind offers and shall inform Tom of them."

The shadow of a smile on the duke's lips deepened. Havergal watched, as if hypnotized. "I hope you brought a tasty hat with you," he warned Crymont.

"Oh damn! Did I smile? I *did*! I felt an unusual twitch in my cheek."

Lettie and Miss FitzSimmons looked on, bewildered. "Surely it is not against the law to smile," Lettie said.

"I never smile," Crymont said categorically, and explained the forfeit. "If I am seen in front of two witnesses to smile, I will be required to eat my hat."

"What wretched conceit," Lettie said, unimpressed. "I am surprised a man in your position must try so hard to gain attention, Your Grace. You do it to draw attention to yourself. All eyes are on you, in hopes of winning the forfeit."

"When one is of diminutive stature, as I am, some pains must be taken to avoid being overlooked."

"Napoleon does not seem to have that difficulty. He, too, is short."

"But I, alas, am not Napoleon. I was not born to

the sword, but to—what *was* I born to, I wonder? Surely I must have an aptitude for something."

"A clown's cap and bells, perhaps?" Havergal suggested. He was unhappy with the duke's hogging of the ladies' attention. He could not imagine why Lettie wasted a moment on him.

"Surely you must have an aptitude for something more positive than not smiling," Lettie said.

Crymont turned a weary eye on Havergal. "You were correct. The lady is unmovable as an oak. I find no pity in her heart. *En effet,* I do not find her heart."

"I don't wear it on my sleeve, Your Grace."

Crymont was in alt at having the undivided attention of the party. He liked that Miss Beddoes took him to task and that Havergal was jealous. He said with a deep look into her eyes, "What must I do to find that elusive organ, madam?"

"You must smile, sir, to show me you appreciate all the advantages Fate has showered on you."

"Done!" he said, and smiled fatuously into her eyes.

Havergal looked on with a grumpy face. "Don't forget to pay the forfeit," he said.

Lettie gave him a knowing glance. "I am surprised at your lack of wits, Havergal. If you really want to see the duke eat his hat, all you had to do was tell him a joke."

"I despise jokes," Crymont said, to return the attention to its proper object.

"Well, that is a great pity," Lettie told him frankly, "for you make yourself an object of humor by playing off these absurd airs and graces. Now, let us speak of something sensible, like dessert."

"I recommend the chantilly," Crymont told her with the glowing eye of infatuation.

The party, though it brought Havergal no closer to his goal, was held to be a great success by the duke. Miss Beddoes liked him; she was not the stiff Tartar Havergal claimed. In short, she would soon be eager to do as he advised her, and he would advise her to hand the thousand pounds over to Havergal.

"I have softened her up for you," he said aside to Havergal when it was time for him to take the ladies home.

"You have done nothing of the sort!" he retorted angrily. He was annoyed at the growing friendship between Lettie and the duke, though he did not consider why it should bother him. "All you have done is show her I consort with *idiots*."

"You won't forget to come back?"

"Then it was a hum that the girls have left?"

"I couldn't tell Miss Beddoes the truth. She would have insisted on the girls joining us. That might have been amusing," he added with a half smile.

"Breaking society's rules is beginning to lose its charm for me. You'll send your carriage and have it waiting at the same place?"

"How soon can you get away?"

"I'll be out the window as soon as we're home. Just give us five minutes so your carriage doesn't overtake us en route."

Havergal found the duke had not impressed Lettie so much as he imagined. Miss FitzSimmons babbled her delight in the dinner party on the way home, but Lettie said, "He is absurd. Imagine a grown man making a wager not to smile, and when he has so much to smile about. I had not realized this vice of wagering is so widespread." Havergal felt it was a dart at himself and said nothing.

Had they been alone, he would have told her he planned to discontinue that style of life. He did plan to change his ways, but he doubted if Lettie would believe him, and he disliked to discuss it in front of Miss FitzSimmons. So he said good night when they returned and went up to his room to climb out the window and meet Crymont's carriage. The meeting seemed an imposition. He would have preferred to go below and talk to the ladies.

Belowstairs, Lettie went about her business. "I must see what the doctor had to say about Jamie's illness," she said, and called the butler.

Siddons came at a stately pace and planted himself in front of her chair. "I am very sorry, ma'am, but there's nothing ails the servants except an overindulgence in wine. Even my own good woman had a tipple in the kitchen. I am hereby tendering our joint resignations, for I won't stay on without her." This piece of bravado was quite ignored.

"What on earth are you saying, Siddons?" Lettie demanded.

"Drunk as lords, the lot of them. It was that carton of wine His Lordship left in the stable for the servants that done the mischief. Cuttle passed around the bottles last night, and they all indulged—to excess, I fear, ma'am."

Lettie stared as if he were insane. "His Lordship left wine for the servants?" she asked in confusion.

"So it seems, ma'am. It was his man Cuttle who doled it out."

"I see," Lettie replied, breathing deeply to control her anger. "Would you be good enough to ask Lord Havergal to step down for a moment. I would like a word with him."

Siddons bowed and left.

"Now Lettie," Miss FitzSimmons said placatingly. "I'm sure there is some good reason. You cannot make a fuss when he has been so nice."

"He has not been nice, Violet. He has behaved *abominably*. How *dare* he encourage my servants in his vices!" She was still ranting five minutes later when Siddons appeared to announce that Lord Havergal was not in his room.

87

"Not in his room? But where is he then?"

"I don't know, ma'am. I have his valet, Cuttle, waiting outside. A trifle the worse for drink, but capable of speech. It was him that fed wine to my missus last night."

"Send him in," Lettie said through thin lips.

Cuttle walked forward with the awful precision of the drunk man trying to appear sober.

Lettie took one glance at his flushed face and bleary eyes and knew his condition. "Where is Lord Havergal? And I'll have no foolish stories," she said angrily.

"He stepped out, mum."

"He did not step out the *door*. I have been here since we reached home."

"He stepped out the window, like."

"Where was he going?"

"To meet the Duke of Crymont, mum."

"I repeat, where?"

"He's putting up at the Royal Oak."

"That is where Havergal went?"

Cuttle shrugged and looked at his slippers. He seemed to have lost one on his way downstairs. Or perhaps he'd forgotten to put both on.

Violet listened closely and thought she had figured it out. She clutched at Lettie's sleeve. "Miss Devereau!" she exclaimed. "He has gone to try to lure Miss Devereau away from the duke, Lettie. How romantic! A runaway match!"

Lettie's heart lurched painfully in her chest, and her cheeks paled.

Cuttle gave Miss FitzSimmons a belligerent stare. "Ho, Miss Devereau, is it? His Lordship ain't one to hoodwink his friends. Miss Devereau is the duke's bit o' muslin. It's a Miss Hardy His Lordship is seeing. A redhead, he says."

Lettie felt she was being consumed with flames from within, yet her outer shell felt like ice. "I see.

You will pack His Lordship's bag and your own and remove them to the front step. When he returns, you will please tell him he is no longer welcome in this house."

Cuttle frowned. "Eh?"

"You heard me. I want Lord Havergal and all his servants and his carriages and his wine out of this house. He is never to darken the door of this house again. Pray tell him I said so, if you can remain sober long enough. Now leave." She lifted a dismissing hand and waved it in Cuttle's direction.

Cuttle shook his head. "He was right. You *are* a Turk," he grumbled, and left to do as he was bid.

Lettie and Violet exchanged a stunned look.

Violet was the first to find speech. "I can't believe it," she said simply. "The nephew of an archbishop. Crymont, I mean."

"I can well believe it. This explains everything. Why we were not introduced to the 'ladies' this afternoon. I wonder that Havergal shrank from *that*, when he has subjected us to every other imaginable indignity. Coming here with his mouth full of lies and his drunken servants. He admitted he wanted his money for gambling. Feeding my servants wine, bringing that wretched duke into our house, pretending those girls had left town."

"I was never so taken in in my life," Violet said quietly.

"Never mind, Violet. He did not succeed in his aim, which was to wheedle his money out of me. Not one penny shall he see till quarter day."

"And we are going to the ball with them tomorrow evening. I cannot think the evening will be at all pleasant."

"Don't be such a peagoose. Of course we are not going to the ball with them."

"But we've arranged the dinner party. . . ."

"We shall have the dinner party. Our guests had to leave early, that is what we shall say."

Violet shook her head sadly. "And they both offered to help Tom out in London. It seemed like such a wonderful opportunity for him. Crymont is Bathurst's godson."

"Crymont is not quite so hateful as Havergal," Lettie said consideringly, for she was quite as alive as Violet to Tom's future. "No doubt Havergal put him up to bringing those girls down here. Crymont had no other reason to come, so far as I can see. Yes, certainly Havergal is leading him astray. I shall tell Tom to call on the duke when he goes up to London but to stay well away from the viscount."

"Do you really think you should leave Havergal's bags at the door, Lettie? That seems a bit harsh."

"I'd like to burn them and throw him on top of the blaze. I never imagined such a deceitful character existed in the whole world. And to think, I was nearly in tears when he said I was old."

"Did he indeed say so?" Violet gasped. "Now, that does not sound like Havergal. He is a trifle wild to be sure, but not *mean*."

"I'm sorry, Miss Beddoes!" Lettie remembered his quick sympathy when he had offended her by saying the simple truth. Something deep within her wanted to find an excuse to forgive him, but common sense prevailed. A hasty word, spoken without thinking, was one thing. But the rest of it, the girls at the inn and the wine—they had been planned in advance. This whole trip had been arranged both for his convenience and for the purpose of conning his money out of her. He wanted her to break her faith to Horace. And even for this one visit, he couldn't do without his debaucheries. The man was a villain. A handsome face wasn't enough to expiate for that.

Chapter Eight

MISS FITZSIMMONS WAS much of a mind to be in her bedroom with the door locked when Lord Havergal returned to find his servants and cases awaiting him on the doorstep. Lettie had no such intention. "I shall be in the saloon with a poker in my hands, ready to fight him off with force if he tries to weasel his way back in," she announced.

"I cannot think he will do anything of the sort."

"We have underestimated his gall before," Lettie said coldly. "I shan't do it again." In any case she wished to hear what he had to say when her message was delivered. This required opening the window an inch, which in turn required wrapping up in a shawl as the night air was chilly. At midnight, they decided to wait in the dark, for Lettie would not give him the satisfaction of knowing he was keeping them up. Violet remained on the scene, with the intention of holding Lettie in check, though she knew perfectly well how ineffectual she would be in a crisis. By one o'clock she was sound asleep, and by two, Lettie had begun to nod off herself.

After waiting up for hours, she missed the initial encounter between Havergal and his waiting servants. Cuttle and Crooks were surprised to see their master approach the front door so early as two o'clock, and relatively sober, too. They were less so themselves. Miss Beddoes had commanded them to remove the wine, and their stomachs seemed the best place to put it.

"What the devil are you two doing out here?" Havergal demanded in surprised accents.

"Waiting for you. We're leaving," Cuttle replied, smiling unsteadily.

"Leaving! What happened?" He laughed. "Did Miss Beddoes catch you pinching the maids?"

It was Havergal's speaking her name that roused Lettie from her doze. She sat bolt upright and moved to the open window to listen from her place of concealment.

"There's none worth pinching," Cuttle replied.

"Did you leave the door on the latch as I asked?" Havergal inquired.

"She locked and bolted it after us."

Havergal felt the first spurt of alarm. "Who did?"

"Cook."

"Ah, then you *were* pinching the servants. Never mind, I'll cross Cook's palm with silver in the morning. Come along. We'll have to get in by a window somehow. And for God's sake, be quiet. We don't want to waken Miss Beddoes."

Miss Beddoes was wide-awake and listening avidly. Bribing her own servants! Was nothing beneath this creature?

"Did you leave my bedroom window open?" Havergal asked.

"I closed it after you slipped out. I was to leave the front door on the latch for you."

"Damn! I'll have to slip around to the kitchen and rouse a servant. Crooks, get those rigs back in the stable, and be quiet about it."

Cuttle rose on unsteady legs. "She said she

wanted you out, bag and baggage. Miss Beddoes did."

"Miss Beddoes!" Havergal exclaimed. An accomplished oath rent the air. Then he said more mildly, "Damn the woman. You'd best tell me exactly what happened."

"She called me down. Asked where you was. I told her."

"You *told* her! Cuttle, you mawworm!"

"She weaseled it out of me."

"I wager your being three sheets to the wind made it easy. She knows I went to the inn, then. I'll tell her I had an emergency message from Crymont. Say his groom delivered it to Crooks, and I didn't mention it as I didn't wish to disturb her. Yes, that'll have to do, and count on an air of innocent bravado to carry it off. I'd best use the front door."

He stepped forward without an instant's hesitation and lifted the knocker. Lettie sat, dumbfounded at what she had just heard. Her first thought was to ignore his knocking and go up to bed. Before she had roused Violet, the knock came again more loudly. It continued, growing more forceful by the second. She pulled her shawl about her and stalked to the front door, poker in hand. She threw the door open wide and glared at him.

He essayed a conning smile and said, "Miss Beddoes. I am most dreadfully sorry to disturb you at this hour."

"Well you might be, Lord Havergal."

"An emergency arose. I had to dash to the inn to help Crymont—"

"I have already heard the explanation with which you mean to con me."

He blinked and frowned, and finally continued uneasily with his explanation. "My groom brought me a message from Crymont's groom. . . ."

"No, milord. You arranged with the duke to steal out of my house for a clandestine meeting with lightskirts at the inn. I know this stunt would pass as a joke in London, another squib in the journals for the *ton* to snicker over, but this is not London. We have higher standards here. The behavior of a lady's houseguest reflects on the hostess. I do not wish to have you under my roof, smuggling wine to my servants, lying, and making a scandal of yourself. To think, I invited the *vicar* to meet you!" she finished, aghast to think of it.

As the first shock subsided, Havergal began trying to think of a polite way out of this morass. As she had discovered about the lightskirts, there seemed little point denying it, so he tried to paint the meeting in less crimson hues. "It was just a friendly meeting. A few hands of cards."

"I am, of course, not so well versed in debauchery as yourself, but I do not believe a gentleman has lightskirts delivered from London for the purpose of playing cards," she said ironically. "You couldn't do without them for *one night*! I was used to think the journals exaggerated about your carrying on, for I could not believe that *anyone* was as bad as they made you seem, but I realize now they showed the simple truth."

Her haughty manner roused his anger, and he answered hotly. "The duke's friends happened to be passing this way."

"There was no need for you to bend the rules of hospitality so hard for the duke's friends. You make the matter worse, not better, by trying to lay the blame in Crymont's dish."

"I am not trying—"

"You waste your breath, Lord Havergal. Any gentleman as indiscreet as yourself ought to hire discreet servants. But then I shouldn't think any self-respecting valet or groom would wish to be in your employ. You are wasting my time and your own. Go back to your harlot. You aren't spending another minute under my roof."

She pushed the door closed. Havergal's hand went out spontaneously to stop it. He had realized the first instant she opened her lips that he hadn't a ghost of a chance of getting his money. It was merely his anger and frustration that he wished to vent now. "That, at least, is a relief," he charged angrily. "I did not come here with any expectation of enjoying myself, but—"

"I know why you came! To try by lies and guile and deceit to extract money before it is due. To take what remains of your fortune and fritter it away on gambling and whoring and God knows what other depravities. Not one penny shall you have. If it were within my powers, I would deny you even your interest."

"I know it very well!" His eyes smoldered, and his nostrils flared. "Any sort of pleasure is anathema to a woman like you. But for all your fine talk, you were not so immune to the flattery and flirtation of a duke. You would have liked well enough to strut into the assembly on his arm. You were eager to flaunt me before your friends this morning as well. I soon realized why you were determined to get me to the village."

"And I realize why you were so eager to keep me out of it! I did not know then that your advantages are limited to a handsome face, sir. I'll be the laughingstock of the village, for it would take more than a title to clothe you in respectability. I dislike your cousin's decision to make me your testamentary guardian, but I see it was necessary he saddle someone with the unenviable task, for you are no more to be trusted than a monkey. My only regret is that I am the unfortunate victim."

"We are both victims in the matter. It has been

no pleasure for me, having my tail under your foot. My cousin's choice could hardly have been worse. You don't know how to enjoy life yourself and are determined that no one else shall."

"You call what you do enjoying life? You don't even know what life is all about, no matter if you have read a little philosophy. You aren't enjoying life, Lord Havergal, you are avoiding it, trying to prolong your childhood into old age. No sense of responsibility, no thought for your future, your character, or your family. I would as lief be guardian to a moonling. In fact, I should prefer it, for at least a moonling has some excuse for his foolish behavior."

"If it is odious to you, I suggest you assign the task of guardian to some objective party," he retaliated, stinging at her attack.

"Someone you can bring around your thumb, you mean. No, Lord Havergal, you are stuck with me, and I am stuck with you, but there is no necessity for further meetings between us. You will receive your quarterly interest and not a penny more till you are thirty. Then you may squander it without bothering my conscience."

Havergal was nearly beyond speech, but he gathered his wits for a last tirade. "You remind me forcibly of an unsavory schoolmaster I once had. How he enjoyed waving his ruler. Give a petty character a little power, and it goes to his head. Don't worry, I shan't trouble you again about this pittance of mine that is temporarily in your control."

"If it is such a pittance, it is strange that you make regular attempts to get hold of it," she retorted.

"As I said, I shan't trouble you again."

He stood back and made an elegant bow, his eyes just glancing off the poker in her hand. "That weapon is unnecessary, ma'am. I never strike a lady, however strong the temptation."

"Something new for you to resist a temptation!" she said, and slammed the door in his face. She went on trembling knees back to the saloon. Violet slept soundly through it all. Lettie heard Havergal stride to the carriage. She heard him bark a few angry commands to his servants, heard the carriages roll down the drive, and sank onto the sofa, exhausted, still holding the poker. She didn't light the lamps, as she wanted concealment. She wasn't crying, but her eyes felt moist from the aftermath of the ordeal.

She was spent, but she had said what she wished to say and didn't regret a word of it. This should put an end to Havergal's importunities. She need not examine the mail for a franked letter every time it was handed to her. She need not go in fear that Havergal discover L. A. Beddoes was a lady. He knew it now, but she doubted he would try to put anything over on her again.

She jiggled Violet's elbow and said, "He's gone, Violet. We can retire now."

Violet sat up, yawning. "Oh, did you speak to him?"

"Yes."

"What did he say?"

"Just the sort of thing we expected, but I put him straight. We'll discuss it in the morning. Let us go upstairs now." She put away the poker and closed the window, all in the dark, then assisted Violet, who was still half-asleep, upstairs.

Lettie thought sleep would come easily now that she had settled the troublesome question of Lord Havergal. She regretted that her dinner party and the assembly would be without its two noble guests. A duke and a viscount would have added a certain dash to them. Havergal was right about one thing.

She had enjoyed taking him on the strut. How her friends had stared! And how they would gossip when word of the lightskirts made the rounds.

As to the rest of his tirade, it was pure nonsense. Saying she didn't know how to enjoy life. She took what enjoyment she could from the small society of the neighborhood. Not everyone had a fortune, a title, and all of London at her feet. She allowed that such perquisites might be enough to turn a young man's head. But that was no excuse for profligacy on the scale practiced by Lord Havergal.

Lord Havergal felt more shame than anger by the time he was in his carriage and on his way to the village. He decided not to put up at the Royal Oak with Crymont. No point adding to the gossip that was no doubt already in circulation. He could disassociate himself somewhat from Cherry and Iona if he at least put up at a different inn. He was the only one who was actually staying with the Beddoes and whose behavior reflected directly on the household.

It was three o'clock by the time he was in his room, but he knew there would be no sleep for him. Miss Beddoes's insults were like thorns in his skin. The sting was sharper for the element of truth in them. Of course the woman was a shrew to be quizzing his servants, but still he regretted that he had left such a poor impression behind him. In her anger she might write to his papa. He was already in poor aroma in that quarter after blowing Uncle Eustace's legacy.

A simple country lady was naturally scandalized at the carrying on of young bucks. He always made a point to behave when he visited his papa and meant to present an equally respectable face at Laurel Hall. Damn Crymont anyway. No one asked him to come along, bringing his wine and wenches and trouble with him. Crymont was half his trouble when you came down to it. He realized that for a childish excuse as soon as it entered his head. But he would definitely drop Crymont.

". . . trying to prolong your childhood into old age. No sense of responsibility, no thought for your future, your character, your family." How often he had heard his papa deliver the same lecture, but this was the first time he had heard the words from a lady, and they troubled him. Damn, youth was the time for sowing wild oats. Everyone knew that. He was still young. He thought Miss Beddoes quite a middle-aged lady though, and she was approximately the same age as himself—twenty-seven. Perhaps he was getting a little old for these pranks. He was three years younger than Crymont in any case.

Crymont was an irreclaimable wastrel. Why did he choose to chum around with the duke? It displeased his father. And it got himself into more hot water than was comfortable. Yes, it was time to put some distance between Crymont and himself. This latest escapade made a good excuse. Crymont knew he was angry with him. He would not hasten to heal the breach. He would only run into greater debt if he kept associating with Crymont and his wild set.

In fact, he might bite the bullet and choose a wife this Season. Twenty-seven seemed a good time for it. He would not choose his bride from any of his current friends. Like all dashers, he preferred a lady of unsullied reputation for matrimony. Almack's was the place to look—if they'd let him in, that is to say. There had been some unpleasantness with Mrs. Drummond Burrell last Season over a clandestine game of faro on the premises—again Crymont's work—but Lady Jersey would vouch for him.

As to his gambling debts, he could not approach

Papa at this time. He must sell off some of his horseflesh. A man didn't need two teams for his carriage and could make do with one hunter and one hacker. His bloods would bring a good price at Tatt's. If he stayed away from the gambling clubs and away from Crymont, he could see it through the Season without troubling his father for more money.

It might be rather amusing to try to skim along on less money. He didn't require any additions to his wardrobe. Papa carried all the expenses of the house in Berkeley Square, including the annual ball that traditionally closed the Season. He also hired a box at Covent Garden, and for the rest of it—invitations to balls, routs, and assemblies were free for the accepting. Why, a man could live on next to nothing if he put his mind to it.

Yes, by Jove, he'd give it a try. He had felt good that morning when he woke early after an early and largely abstemious night. It would be pleasant not to wake with a fuzzy head, a dry throat, and a vague worry as to how he had misspent his night. He might start a whole new regime: morning rides in Rotten Row where he'd meet all the debs, afternoon drives in the park and social calls, polite parties at night. And it would keep him clear of Crymont.

The only pity of it was that Miss Beddoes would not hear of his having turned over a new leaf. . . .

Chapter Nine

THE LAST THAT was heard from the noble visitors to Ashford was a note from the Duke of Crymont, delivered at noon the following day by His Grace's footman. The duke penned a pretty apology, taking blame for the whole imbroglio and begging Miss Beddoes's pardon. He implored that she not blame Lord Havergal for anything but an excess of eagerness to oblige his friend. Lord Havergal, he stressed, was not aware that the females in question were coming to town and had tried to avoid meeting them. It was the duke himself who had left wine for the servants. No note was received from Lord Havergal.

"At least *one* of them is a gentleman," Lettie sniffed, after scanning His Grace's note. "Havergal has conned Crymont into taking all the blame. I think we might ask Tom to call on the duke without fear, Violet, when he goes to London."

Violet read the note and agreed heartily. "Indeed, he might. The duke is very polite. And as you said, Lettie, why should he have come scrambling all the way to Ashford if Havergal had not asked him to? He could have consorted with those women in London. It was all Havergal's doing, though I'm sure he meant no harm. Youthful enthusiasm, you know, and London habits," she said forgivingly. Lettie just looked at her askance.

Such infamous carrying on as the noblemen had treated Ashford to was much discussed and analyzed. The gossip lent some liveliness to an otherwise uneventful dinner party the next evening. Mrs. Smallbone had learned from the proprietor of the Royal Oak what viands the party of four had consumed at their orgy, and what wines accompanied it. "Nothing but champagne, which the duke brought with him, and a good thing he did, too, for the Royal Oak would have nothing to equal it, I warrant."

The absence of the duke and the viscount from the assembly was felt severely. The local ladies, in particular, were reduced to a pulp, for they had been looking forward to being seduced in such high style. It was whispered behind raised hands that Miss Beddoes was jealous as a green cow, and what did she expect? That she could bribe Lord Havergal into marrying her only because she held his purse strings? Mr. Norton's sorrow was no less than the ladies'. "I think you were a bit hard on the lads, Miss Lettie" was his comment.

He was resplendent in a new evening suit for the assembly. A jacket of sapphire blue velvet set out a mile on his wadded shoulders. In his cravat a ruby twinkled, as like to Crymont's as was available in Ashford.

"I wanted to discuss pig racing with Havergal," he said disconsolately. "It sounded an excellent new notion to me. He was to call on me at the swinery. I would have taken him to Norton Knoll for dinner, of course," he added. "I have even put in a bid on the Chester White. I shall write the viscount to learn the ins and outs of it all. With no jockeys, there must be some method of holding the swine at the starting gate and getting them started. Could you give me his address, Miss Lettie? I'll invite him for a visit."

After several efforts to dissuade him, Lettie could see no way out of it and gave him the address.

"If, by any chance, Lord Havergal accepts your invitation, I pray you will not bring him to call on me," she said.

"You were too hard on the lad, Miss Lettie. The royals will have their fun."

"Lord Havergal is not a member of the royal family," she pointed out.

"Just so. I meant the nobility, of course. Same thing, so far as social doings go. They all take their lead from the prince. I heard the ladies in question were the height of fashion. A blonde and a red-head."

"I have not heard of the prince racing pigs," Lettie said dampingly.

"He hasn't the wits to come up with a new twist, poor lad. He is a follower, but insofar as squandering blunt and womanizing goes, they are all cut from the same bolt. The only difference is that we taxpayers must pay the prince's baker, whereas Havergal and Crymont foot their own bills. It is nothing to us, after all, how they wish to spend their own money. I buy what I wish and ask no one's permission."

"But you don't waste your money, Mr. Norton. Except perhaps on that Chester White," she added.

"It is a vexation for you, looking after Havergal's legacy," he conceded. "I don't know why you don't just turn the trust over to his papa. It is clear old Cauleigh holds a tight set of reins. He would not let the lad have his way with the money."

This struck Lettie as a sound idea. She doubted it was his father Havergal had in mind as a replacement when he suggested she quit the trust, and it gave her some satisfaction to outwit him in this way. Why should she be pestered when Havergal was nothing to her? Any hope of adding luster to her own family by the connection was gone. She had no desire to see him again, she would not let Tom near the man, so why continue with the unpleasant job? The next morning, she wrote a short note to Lord Cauleigh, expressing the sentiment that handling Sir Horace's legacy had become burdensome, and at Lord Havergal's suggestion she wished to terminate it. Who more logical than Lord Cauleigh himself, who already had charge of the majority of Havergal's monies, to take over?

Lord Cauleigh received the note and pondered over it. He had been given a high opinion of Miss Beddoes from his Cousin Horace. What had Havergal done to upset her? Got himself into debt, very likely, and tried to get hold of that twenty-five thousand pounds. It was not to be thought of. Lord Cauleigh usually made one foray to London each spring, to visit his old friends and catch up with what was going forward at the House of Lords. He decided to make the visit before replying to Miss Beddoes.

He was agreeably surprised to find his son not only sober and dining at home, but expressing the intention of attending the opening do at Almack's that evening. Havergal looked particularly well. The clear eye and healthy visage across the table from him held no suggestion of excessive drinking or carousing.

"How are you fixed for money, Jacob?" he inquired warily.

"I'm fine, Papa." His son smiled. "In fact, I have sold off a few of my surfeit horses and would like you to accept five hundred pounds for the Cauleigh Orphanage. I hope to give you another five hundred next quarter day."

"Indeed!" his father exclaimed, shocked. "It seems you have turned over a new leaf. I am very happy to hear it."

"I have decided it is time to settle down, Papa. I am thinking of marrying and would like to ask your opinion as to a suitable bride. Perhaps you will accompany me to Almack's this evening?"

This sounded so unlike his son that Cauleigh could only stare. "Indeed!" he said, and felt a horrible foreboding of disaster. The lad was deeply dipped and was looking about for a fortune to marry.

"I trust this five hundred you speak of did not come from post-obits, Jacob?"

His son looked up, startled. "Why no, Papa. I told you, I sold off some of my horses."

"Aye, I heard what you said," his father replied, unconvinced. "I also know that you have been pestering poor Miss Beddoes for money. I have had a note from her."

"What!" Havergal's face turned pink, and his eyes sparkled angrily. "I don't see why she had to pester you about that. What—what did she say?" he asked warily. It seemed hard that his old sins should be thrown in his face just when he had undertaken a serious reformation.

"She wishes me to take over the handling of Horace's legacy. I can only conclude you have been importuning her for funds. In fact, I know you have been talking to her."

Havergal's jaws clenched. So she had gone running to tattle to his father. Just what he might have expected! "You must not believe everything the lady says, Papa. There were extenuating circumstances."

"She says you expressed the notion of her giving up the handling of the trust, and whatever you have

105

done, she is eager to be rid of you. Would you have me believe Miss Beddoes is untruthful?"

"I may have expressed the idea in the heat of argument."

His father's brow darkened. "What did you find to argue about? Miss Beddoes has behaved scrupulously in this entire matter. She was not at all eager to undertake the job."

"It had little to do with the money, actually."

"Then perhaps you will tell me what it *had* to do with?"

"I would prefer not to, Papa," he said, and regretted he had laid himself open to the question. Miss Beddoes had not given him away, then.

"I trust you did not make improper advances to the lady?"

"To Miss Beddoes!" he exclaimed, staring in horror. "I am not so brave, Papa."

Lord Cauleigh assumed a serving wench had been led astray, and said angrily, "If you cannot behave like a gentleman, Jacob, I beg you will not intrude yourself into polite households. Have some concern for your family's reputation if you have none for your own."

Havergal clamped his lips and swallowed the name, Crymont. It wasn't all the duke's fault. He didn't have to go to the inn. "Nothing of that sort occurred at Laurel Hall," he said stiffly. That was true in word if not in spirit. All the trouble had occurred at the inn and outside Miss Beddoes's house.

"I expect you are still rattling around town with Crymont's set" was Lord Cauleigh's next conversational effort after he had finished his soup.

"Very little, Papa. I only meet him by chance occasionally, for he goes about a good deal, you know."

"Thank God for that! The lad will run through

one of the finest fortunes in the country. I would dislike my son to accompany him on that journey. Conceited popinjay! What was the meaning of that squib, showing him eating his hat? Some silly wager, I daresay."

The wager sounded so excessively silly that Havergal was ashamed to state it. "As I said, I am seeing less of Crymont. I am not up on his latest follies."

Over a plate of turbot in white sauce, the subject of Horace's legacy arose again. "About Miss Beddoes, Papa, will you take over the trust?" Havergal inquired.

"If you wish, but it will do you no good. You will not find me a softer touch than Miss Beddoes."

"No, I do not wish it," Havergal said thoughtfully. He wanted to fulfill his proud boast and not ask Miss Lettie for money again. How would she know he had reformed if she was not in charge of the trust? He wanted to show her he was not so lost as she believed. Some irrevocable regret lingered at the back of his mind that she had such a poor opinion of him. He had not behaved as a gentleman should.

"I won't have you annoying the lady, Jacob. You must *promise* me you will not be pestering her for interest before it is due."

"I have no intention of pestering her."

"I shall ask her to notify me if you do."

Havergal gave an angry glare, but as the meal progressed, he decided that cut was well deserved. He had failed to live up to his promises before now. A fine state of affairs when a man's own father couldn't believe him!

"Have you decided about Almack's, Papa?"

"Yes, I shall accompany you. If you are serious about marriage, we must have a look at the market. Lord Dunstan's daughter is making her bows. A good dowry there. Thirty-five thousand, I hear."

Havergal knew as soon as the name was out that he was not interested in marrying Lady Anne, not if she had thirty-five million pounds.

They proceeded to Almack's after dinner, suitably attired in knee breeches, white cravats, and chapeau bras. Havergal feared he was going to be barred from entering. Mrs. Drummond Burrell's face froze implacably and did not defrost until Lord Cauleigh stepped forward. Havergal skated in on his father's coattails.

"You are aware, Lord Havergal, that gambling is held at a minimum, and only orgeat is served," she said coldly.

"I have an excellent memory, ma'am," he assured her.

"It is not your *memory* that concerns me," she said, and glided away.

A few other ladies besides Lady Anne were brought forward for inspection. Miss Heatherington had a prettier face, but a smaller dot and an annoying habit of agreeing with every word uttered, no matter how inane. Havergal thought of Glaucon and inevitably of Miss Beddoes. No excess of agreement in that quarter! How the shrew liked to argue. The only two ladies Havergal really found interesting were a dashing widow encumbered with two children and a heavy burden of debt, and Lady Selden, who possessed great conversational skills, a lively countenance, and a perfectly healthy young husband. He had always preferred the conversation of older ladies. Miss Beddoes had been conversable. . . .

"What brings you here, Havergal?" Lady Selden asked archly. "Has Papa lowered the ax? Marry, or you are cut off?"

"You mistake the matter, ma'am. It is I who have brought Papa."

She laughed merrily. "Yes, and it is the heat that brings the sun. Come now, confess. What heinous impropriety have you indulged in that your father is riding herd on you, rogue? I am not easily shocked. It must be something really hot if the journals are afraid to touch it."

"I am not involved in any heinous impropriety! I don't think I care for your choice of words, Countess."

She looked offended. "This is something new, to see Havergal on his high horse! I had not realized you were capable of being shocked."

"You make me sound like a—a rake, or a wastrel!"

"Only because you usually behave like one." She laughed. "Come now, don't go sanctimonious on us. You were used to be more amusing."

Is that what he had sunk to, something to amuse the *ton*? Like a monkey, or the village innocent, or a freak. Every lady he spoke to expressed astonishment to see him at this sedate do. When had his reputation become so scarlet? He undertook to repair it by dancing with all the antidotes and two of the patronesses, and had a dreadful evening.

But he felt he deserved it and took a sort of painful pleasure in paying for his crimes. Let society see he was no longer their toy, someone to set them laughing and pointing. Like any reformed rake, he became quite censorious in his outlook and glared at those who left early to go on to livelier dos.

"We're off to Brook's, Havergal. Interested in joining us?" a friend asked. Mr. Barton was one of the year's leading Corinthians.

"No, I am staying till the end."

"We'll make your apologies. I daresay your papa

109

will not be making a long visit in town," Barton commiserated.

Fools! Going to squander their money. He knew that Barton was playing on tick at Brook's, and how did he hope to pay up without selling his estate? The man was mad.

He was up early in the morning for a ride in the park, and when he returned, his father was just leaving for the House.

"Is something important being discussed that you have come to town to attend?" Havergal asked.

His father said, "I know you do not see fit to exercise the privilege of attending the sessions at the House, Jacob, but I had hoped you at least *read* what is afoot in your own country. Mills and factories shutting down because of tariff restrictions on our goods, hundreds of thousands of discharged soldiers looking for work, and the heavy taxes levied to pay for Napoleon's war making investment difficult—yes, I would say something important will be discussed. How to keep our population from starving to death! I ought to be attending full time, but one of us must keep an eye on affairs at home. I hope you enjoyed your ride in the park."

Lord Cauleigh clamped his curled beaver on his head and left. Havergal went to the saloon and sank into a comfortable sofa. There was no pleasing Papa! And at the back of his mind, he felt there was no pleasing Miss Lettie either. Just so would she have ripped up at him. Damn, he was leaving off all his old bad habits. What did they expect?

His father obviously expected he should waste these beautiful spring days sitting on a hard chair at Whitehall. Or had there been a hint in there that he ought to be at the Willows, handling their own estate? Papa was getting a bit old for it, of course. It was a large estate. Damn, what use would he be at home? He knew nothing of farming. And nothing of politics either. He hadn't seen any signs of this poverty his father spoke of.

He lifted the journal his father had been reading and glanced through it. It all seemed to be true. He read harrowing tales of thousands of ex-soldiers starving. There were stories of riotous meetings in the provinces—Manchester, Littleport, Nottingham. It was bound to spread to London. Visions of a revolution along the lines of the recent French Revolution reeled in his head. When had all this begun? Why had no one told him? He dashed to the door and called for his carriage. His father was astonished and gratified to see Havergal enter the House an hour later.

Something had awakened the lad's conscience. Nothing was as likely to have done it as a lady. Cauleigh tugged at his chin, wondering who the lady could be. Perhaps Miss Beddoes knew something about this. He would drop by Laurel Hall on his way home and have a word with her.

Chapter Ten

IN ASHFORD, THERE was a fire at the vicarage, which cast the memory of Havergal and the duke into limbo. Like everyone else, Lettie and Violet drove into the village the next day to offer help and see the ruins, not necessarily in that order. When they returned, they were told a gentleman was waiting to see them.

Lettie found it hard to believe that the quiet, well-bred, harried, and really not at all handsome lord sitting in her saloon could be Havergal's papa. How had this austere gentleman given birth to such a comet as Havergal? It surpassed all understanding.

"Was there any particular reason why you wish to be rid of the trust, Miss Beddoes?" he inquired, after he had been given a glass of wine, and the purpose of his visit was revealed.

"The idea came from your son. It struck me as a good one."

"Buy why? I cannot think the quarterly writing of a check is what distresses you. Come now, tell the truth. I am the lad's father. What has he done?"

Loath as she was to reveal Havergal's sins, Lettie knew some excuse must be given. She said vaguely, "Our correspondence was more frequent than that, Lord Cauleigh. Havergal often requests advances that are not in keeping with your cousin Horace's intentions. He can be quite insistent."

"I know it well," he admitted. "He was used to harass me in the same way, till I put my foot down. You have only to give him a categorical no, and that will be the end of it."

"I believe I did that the last time."

"Has he bothered you since?"

"No, but that was only ten days ago. I have no doubt—"

"I believe you may be mistaken. Jacob—Havergal—has turned over a new leaf. He has left off seeing a certain set of wild bucks and taken his seat in the House. That will keep him out of mischief while he is in town, and at the Season's close, he tells me he plans to come to Willow Hall."

"Do you believe this improvement will last?" she asked bluntly.

"I do, for I believe there is a lady at the bottom of it. He mentioned marriage, yet each lady I brought forth was rejected. It is my belief that he has already made up his mind, and it is for her that he is reforming. Jacob was always more easily led by a lady than anyone else. His mama's influence—they were close. The same warm, excitable temper and good looks, but she knew how to handle him. It was when she died that he went to the bad. Pity. If the match he has in his eye is a lady of character, I expect she turned him off, and he is out to show her he can be as upstanding as the next fellow. Why else would he go to Almack's? It is my intention to encourage this liaison if the lady is even so much as genteel."

Lettie listened with keen interest and just a little heaviness of the heart. So Havergal was reforming to please a lady. Who could she be? She must be some Incomparable to tame that rake. "What has that to do with my keeping the trust?" she asked.

"Only that I do not think Havergal will bother you much in the future. I am pretty busy, between Willow Hall and the House, and the change would involve meetings with lawyers and a deal of paperwork. It will only be for two and a half years more."

Lettie considered it a moment and took her decision. It seemed hard to refuse this tired old man. "Very well, if you wish it, Lord Cauleigh, I'll give it another try."

"You are very obliging, ma'am. Before I leave, there is just one other thing that mystifies me. This hypothetical lady, would you have any idea who she might be? Jacob does not visit her in London. I thought the trip to Almack's must be to see her, but if so, she was not there. I know he visited you recently. Did he meet some lady hereabouts? Naturally, I am curious to learn what I can of her background."

"He met no ladies here except myself and my companion, Miss FitzSimmons," she replied, nodding to Violet, who listened with wide eyes to the whole.

"You do not think it could be Miss Hardy, Miss Devereau's friend!" Violet exclaimed. "Oh dear. That would never do."

"Is there something 'amiss with the lady?" Lord Cauleigh asked eagerly.

"The women Miss FitzSimmons speaks of are not ladies, milord," Lettie said, pink with embarrassment.

"Ah! Then we can rule them out. Jacob's character is not all one could wish, but he is not an utter fool. He would never offer for a lightskirt. Perhaps I am mistaken in thinking a lady is involved."

"The only ladies he met were Miss Beddoes and myself," Violet repeated.

Cauleigh examined them, Violet first, then Miss Beddoes. A question formed in his mind. Miss Beddoes? A little old, but then Jacob had never really cared for debs. And why had Jacob not wanted Miss Beddoes to give up the trust? That was odd. She was not a bad-looking woman. A little stiff-rumped for Jacob, but there was no saying.

"Perhaps it is one of you ladies he has in his eye," he said, making it a joke, but watching Lettie closely. He saw the color flood her cheeks, and his interest soared.

"He did not care in the least for me," Lettie said firmly. "I'm afraid I was required to read him a lecture before he left. It must be you, Violet," she said, smiling at her friend, to ease her way out of the embarrassing situation.

Violet laughed uneasily and said, "Mr. Norton invited him to Norton Knoll. Perhaps he met someone there, Lettie."

"I don't believe Havergal ever paid the visit. Mr. Norton would have told us so if that were the case," Lettie pointed out. She turned to Cauleigh and added, "Mr. Norton raises hops and pigs. It was the pigs that your son had some interest in."

"Indeed! That is odd, for we don't raise pigs at home. We keep cattle." Lettie said not a word about pig racing.

Before long Lord Cauleigh took his departure. So Jacob had come to cuffs with Miss Beddoes. That was a promising sign. He would not have lost his temper if he had not been emotionally involved. He would have poured on the charm and oiled his way around her. She must be a remarkably strong lady to have withstood his begging for money all these months. This romance, if romance it was, must be encouraged in some manner. He went home to Willow Hall to think out a scheme.

"What do you make of that?" Violet asked when the ladies were alone.

"I hope Lord Cauleigh knows what he is talking about, for the only woman Havergal had in his eye when he was here was that redhead lightskirt."

"Her name was Iona Hardy," Violet supplied quite unnecessarily. The name was etched in Lettie's mind.

"If he is thinking of marrying her—"

"His papa said he would not."

"I doubt his father knows anything about Havergal. It wouldn't surprise me in the least," Lettie declared.

"Such a shame! It would have been so much more romantic if he could have fallen in love with you, Lettie."

Lettie turned a scalding eye on her companion. "Much good it would have done him."

"You cannot be entirely immune to him! So handsome, and rich, and a title."

"I was never one to hanker after wealth and a title. Now, to business. What is to be done about Mr. Norton's public day? He wants you and me to give him a hand." Lettie allowed herself one small pang of regret that Havergal had not been interested in her. He did have such a charming smile and such liveliness. It seemed he was capable of reforming for the right woman.

In the middle of May, Lord Havergal was requested to pay a visit to Willow Hall, and to his father's surprise, he agreed without argument. After a few weeks of reading newspapers, listening to alarming reports of poverty and riots in the House, and touring the less affluent parts of London to check out matters for himself, Havergal was struck as never before by the opulence of his ancestral home. A winding road led through acres of cultivated park to a noble heap of stone, arranged in the style of Queen Anne, that covered an acre. How lovely it looked with the windows gleaming gold in the setting sun. How fortunate a creature he was, and he had never given a moment's thought to it, except to waste the wealth he had been given.

"Stable this rig, Crooks," he said. "And you, Cuttle—I want to see you run two tours around this park before you lay out my evening clothes. You have a match coming up next week."

All Havergal's servants were carried along in the great reformation. Cuttle was on a Spartan regime: up at seven, run for an hour, work out at Jackson's gym, and frequently with his master. Fun was not entirely omitted from Havergal's life, but it was taking a different, healthier turn.

"What was it you wished to see me about, Papa?" he asked when they met in Lord Cauleigh's study for sherry before dinner. Various relatives were either living or visiting at Willow Hall, and dinner would give them no privacy.

"I am thinking of setting up a small pig farm, Jacob. If a man of my age doesn't dabble in new things occasionally, he becomes bored. Would any of your chums be in that line? I know you have extensive acquaintances. I thought you might visit one of them and learn something about it firsthand." He listened sharply. If the name Norton arose when Havergal's close friends, the Gowers, had an excellent pig farm in this same county, he would know.

Havergal rubbed his chin and frowned. "Curious you should mention that, Papa. It happens I met a chap last month. Fellow by the name of Norton, in Kent, and he invited me to call on him. He is quite an expert—well worth the trip, I think."

"Indeed! That is fortunate. When would you be able to get away?"

"I can go anytime. That is to say, I am on the committee working to lower the tariffs on the importation of grains, but I daresay they can spare me for a few days."

"Perhaps you should write to this Norton and see when it will be convenient for you to go."

"I'll do it this very night. What sort of pigs are you interested in, Papa? Would it be lard, bacon, or fresh pork?"

Cauleigh had no more notion of pigs than he had of lightskirts. "Let us hope your friend, Norton, can tell us which is the most profitable and the least trouble."

Havergal wrote off his letter that same evening and sent it by his own footman, mounted on a fast nag. No letter ever gave its recipient such bliss since Abelard penned his famous epistles to Eloise. Norton sent back his reply with the messenger, stating that his time was completely at Lord Havergal's disposal and that he would be thrilled and honored to receive His Lordship. Lord Havergal was packed and waiting and left as soon as he had his reply.

As Norton was such a bosom bow of Lettie's—not a potential suitor, surely?—there was a high probability of meeting her. There would be some initial embarrassment, but she would soon see he had changed. They might drive out one day or attend an assembly to make up for the one he had missed. He had no intention of falling in love with Miss Beddoes. She was too tyrannical for him, but he knew he had behaved badly and wished for her good opinion. She was the sort of woman he ought to be looking for as a wife, only younger and more agreeable, of course, and well dowered.

Norton wanted to share his good fortune with the

whole world. His first port of call was always Laurel Hall, and he went thither as soon as he had informed Miss Millie of the impending visit.

Soon Siddons shuffled to the door and announced, "Mr. Norton, ma'am."

Norton came striding in, filling the room with his vitality and self-consequence.

"You have come to discuss your public day, Mr. Norton," Violet said. She unconsciously patted the seat beside her as she spoke, but it was to the chair beside Lettie that he sped.

"That, too," he said, and could not hold in his marvelous news a second longer. "I have had a letter from Lord Havergal. He is coming to visit me to look over my swinery."

Lettie and Violet exchanged a startled look. "Indeed!" Lettie said in a weak voice. Her heart pounded with what she told herself was annoyance. Yet it was a very eager annoyance. "When do you expect him?"

"Any day now. He was most eager."

"Don't lend him any money," Lettie said, "or invest in anything he may be promoting."

Norton leaned forward. "Do you figure that's what he's up to? I own I found it a little odd."

"I cannot think why else he would come."

"I figured it was the pig-racing venture. He was keen on that, if you mind. I'll bear your caution in mind, Miss Lettie. Now what Miss Millie wants me to find out is how we must entertain him. Dinner parties every evening, of course, and a ball. She quite depends on you ladies to lend her a hand, for she's never entertained anyone higher than a member, and old Limpy Savarin is no better than ourselves."

"Neither is Lord Havergal," Lettie said firmly. "You are doing him a favor to let him come. No extraordinary efforts need be made at entertainment."

"I daresay he will keep his piece at the Royal Oak again and entertain himself." No accent of censure tinged this speech, but rather something like admiration. "I wonder if the duke will be joining him. He didn't say so. What I had in mind was to rush the public day forward and hope to squeeze it in while he is here."

"I see no reason to inconvenience the whole village by changing the date," Lettie objected.

"Inconvenience them? Nay, the lasses will be thrilled to pieces. You mind how they were close to tears when Lord Havergal and the duke shabbed off on our assembly. The gals will get to flaunt their finery in front of them yet." In his mind it was half-settled that the duke would be along.

Violet said, "Did you say you were having a ball, Mr. Norton?"

"At least one," he said, wild with abandon.

"Oh my! Did you hear that, Lettie? A ball!"

"Yes, I heard it, but as to lending Miss Millie a hand, I fear we are quite busy just now, Mr. Norton."

"I'm not busy! I'll help!" Violet announced. "I should love it."

"What has suddenly filled your time, Miss Lettie?" Norton asked suspiciously.

"I am always busy in the spring," she said vaguely. "The garden . . ."

Norton shook his head at this poor excuse. "There is no point thinking you can avoid the lad entirely, Miss Lettie. Best to shake hands and let bygones be bygones. You cannot sit across from him at the table every night and glower in silence."

"We have not accepted any invitations to dinner."

"Of course you will come," he said simply. And

of course they would. Such social activities as he spoke of were too rare to pass up on a mere matter of principle. Violet would certainly attend, and it would be too noticeable if Lettie refused to accompany her. Lettie wouldn't miss the ball for all the money in the Bank of England, and if she was to attend that, then why miss out on the rest?

And if Norton was to entertain on this grand scale, it would be as well to help Miss Millie, or she would run amok with her exuberant bad taste and import a load of French chefs to construct ice sculptures and inedible French dishes.

Mr. Norton was eager to be off, spreading his good news far and wide and beginning his preparations. "I'll send the carriage for you tomorrow at two, ladies. Now I must be off to the shop to buy invitation cards. Gold-edged, do you think?"

"Plain white, Mr. Norton," Lettie said, and realized that she really must be on hand, or the Nortons would make laughingstocks of them all.

"What a nuisance," Lettie said after Mr. Norton had gone. Then she bent over her sewing to conceal an errant smile.

"Yes indeed," Violet said automatically, but her heart was bouncing with excitement and so was Lettie's. "We must have new gowns for that ball, Lettie. Let us nip into Ashford and speak to Miss Dawson. She will be overwhelmed with work."

"I do not plan to buy a new gown to impress Lord Havergal," Lettie said grandly, but she dashed for her pelisse. New lace was imperative and perhaps some new ribbons for her old gown. . . . Havergal had never seen it; it would be as good as a new gown to him. She would wear Mama's diamonds that she valued so, and which she found so little opportunity to show off.

Chapter Eleven

Norton's CARRIAGE ARRIVED for the ladies early the
next afternoon and carried them off to Norton
Knoll. An eager Mr. Norton and a somewhat less
keen Miss Millie were waiting for them in the glittering splendor of the red saloon. Lettie never entered the chamber without a wince, to see so much
money lavished to achieve such vulgarity. Anything that was not red velvet or brocade was gilt.
Miss Millie really ought to provide green glasses to
counteract the dazzling brilliance of the ten or
twelve lamps burning in bright daylight.

One's first impression of Miss Millie was that she
was made up of eyes, hair, and bones. She was a
gaunt lady, whose dark eyes fairly popped out of
her face. Like her saloon, Miss Millie's toilette was
a study in rococo splendor. The russet-gray hair
around her face was tortured into a surfeit of curls,
the gown covering her body was festooned in bows,
buttons, and lace, and the whole gown was topped
with a bunch of garnet brooches.

"What do you make of this then, ladies?" she
greeted them, proud in her litany of complaints.
"Norton has gone and invited Lord Havergal for a
visit. I'm sure I don't know how I shall cope, for we

never had a noble head gracing our table before. No idea when he is coming, who he is bringing with him, how long he is staying, or whether he will want to stay here or at the cottage to be near the pigs, for his excuse is that he wants to talk to Ned about pigs. And how shall we entertain him?" She looked in awful desperation to Lettie for a reply.

"If he is coming to study, then he is not here to be entertained," Lettie said. "Feed him, introduce him to your friends, and let nature take its course. Perhaps Havergal will have his own ideas of what entertainment he wishes, and no doubt your neighbors will issue invitations."

"So kind of you, Miss Lettie. Ned said I might count on you. Just let me know what evening you will be ready to take him off our hands for dinner."

Lettie stared, but before she could contradict this idea, Mr. Norton, who had been smiling indulgently at his sister's excitement, took the floor. "You've hit it on the head, Miss Lettie. Havergal might very well bring along his own amusement and keep her at the Royal Oak. I trust he wouldn't try to foist his bit o' muslin off on us."

"That was not my meaning!" Lettie exclaimed, though as she considered the past, it did not seem at all improbable.

"I wonder if he will bring the duke with him," Norton said musingly. "If he comes, Miss Millie, you must give the duke the best guest suite and put Havergal in the acorn suite. Noblesse oblige," he added in a knowing aside to Miss FitzSimmons.

Lettie perked up her ears. She had frequently reviewed her meeting with Lord Cauleigh, and between her and Violet it was a settled thing that the wild set of friends Havergal had dropped included Crymont. "Did he mention bringing the duke?" she asked sharply. It immediately occurred to her that he was coming to Ashford to do the things he dared not do in London for fear of his father hearing about them.

"No, it was only a short note," Norton said sadly. "Miss Millie has got it put away among her souvenirs, but he did not mention the duke. I read in the *Observer* this morning, however, that the Duke of C. and a string of little stars were still racing porkers in Green Park, so likely he will come. It is this business of pig racing that brings Havergal, of course."

All this boded ill for the tale of Havergal's having reformed. Lettie concluded he had pulled the wool over his papa's eyes, likely for the purpose of conning him out of the thousand pounds to pay his gambling debts. She was sorry to hear it and hardened her heart against him. If she wished to see any of her neighbors during the length of his visit, however, she could not refuse to come to Norton's house. Indeed, it would be a slight against this old friend to refuse, but she would not issue any invitations of her own, and she would be cool to Havergal.

"Well, shall we get to work?" she suggested.

"I have had a table set up with paper and pens and calendars in the morning parlor," Norton said. "I thought we might block out the days and evenings, and see what we can find to fill them with."

"And menus," Miss Millie added, for the meals were her particular duty.

The party retired to the morning parlor, where fresh coffee and cakes awaited them. Each place at the table was set up with an array of papers, pens, and its own individual calendar, as though they were planning not a simple visit, but a schedule for the invasion of France.

Norton sat at the head of the table and arranged his stationery. "The first item of business is the day of arrival. I figure he'll land in around dinnertime, for he'll make the dart in one day. What we must decide is how to get a party together on short notice, since we don't know what day he will be coming. I begin to think that what we must do is have a large dinner party every evening until he gets here."

Violet laughed out loud and received a rebukeful glare from Norton.

"In such a case of uncertainty, I should wait till the next evening to begin festivities," Lettie suggested. "Havergal will be tired after his trip and will not want a late evening." Mr. Norton objected to this meager sort of hospitality, and Lettie added, "Very likely you will have a note from him setting the day and approximate time of arrival. He would think it odd if he arrived unexpected and found a large party awaiting him."

"We don't want to give him the notion we are *odd* the minute he gets here," Miss Millie warned Norton.

"True, true. We don't want to give the lad the idea we've never entertained nobility before."

Lettie encouraged this point of view. "Too much concern for his entertainment would be just a shade vulgar," she said.

"Aye, but on the other hand, we shan't serve him bread pudding either," he retaliated with a sharp look.

They got down to ransacking their minds for people to invite to the various parties Norton intended to hold. Miss Lettie and Miss Violet headed each list, till Lettie called him to account.

"It would be better to vary your guests, Mr. Norton. Lord Havergal will not want to see the same faces every evening."

"You mean I cannot attend all the parties, when I shall have all the work?" Miss Millie demanded.

"No indeed, ma'am. Naturally you, as hostess,

125

must sit at the foot of your brother's table for all the festivities. And Lord Havergal should sit at Mr. Norton's right hand," she added, lest this detail had escaped notice.

"Then he will be looking at the same spot on the wall every night," Millie announced. "And it is that old painting of the dead partridges and guns he will be looking at, too. They are enough to put anyone off his feed."

"We'll change it each night," Norton said, and added this absurdity to his list.

Miss Millie took advantage of his writing to say, "You must tell me what local girls I could hire for the duration, Miss Lettie, and some idea what elegant additions to add to the pork." Pork replaced mutton as a synonym for dinner in this household.

Lettie gave her suggestions and promised to send over receipts for her more esoteric dishes. The meeting had just entered "Wine" on their list, when the butler appeared at the door.

"Lord Havergal," he announced, and behind him loomed the well-remembered form of that gentleman. The group sat in stunned silence, staring as if he were a wild beast.

Lettie felt the breath catch in her lungs. In her mind the bitter nature of her memories had blunted the edges of his beauty. She had not thought his eyes could really be so bright and so long-lashed. His complexion had a healthy glow, his smile was enchanting, and his tailoring, as usual, was impeccable. He executed a graceful bow and entered nonchalantly.

"I feel as if I'm interrupting a meeting of the Cabinet. I'll retire, and let you honorable members get on with whatever you're doing. Parish work, is it?" His eyes quickly toured the group before settling on Lettie. Their eyes met for one electric instant, before she lowered her gaze.

Now why the deuce was she blushing? That girl-ish blush and new air of uncertainty were becoming to her. Made her seem younger and not so demmed stiff-rumped as before.

Norton sprang to his feet, shuffling his papers into a folder as if they held plans for treason. Havergal noticed the movement, and he noticed as well that a warning glance to the others caused them all to do the same thing. What the devil had he stumbled into here? Some sort of village conspiracy?

"Lord Havergal! Delighted to see you," Norton said, and went to the door to lead him to the saloon. The ladies rose and followed. "We didn't look to see you for a few days yet."

"I ought to have written first, but Papa is very eager to get on with his new idea of raising hogs. If I have come at an awkward time, please don't pay me the least heed. I can go on at once to your pig farm, and your man there can show me around." He stopped at the saloon doorway and blinked at the lavish red and gold panorama before him. The words "Brighton Pavilion" darted into is head. A closer look told him there was nothing oriental in the decor, but the overall effect was similarly blinding.

"Nonsense! Nothing would give me greater pleasure than to show you around myself," Norton assured him.

"But you seemed so busy." Lettie and Havargal entered and found seats. Lettie was careful to put herself at the maximum remove possible from Havergal, while still remaining within hearing distance.

"The ladies are helping me make plans for my public day. I hope you will be here for it. A week from tomorrow it is to be held. We were hoping that your friend, the duke, could be persuaded to come as well."

"I had not planned to batten myself on you for quite so long as that. Two or three days . . ."

"A month is more like it, to learn all the tricks of the trade." Norton pulled the cord, and a footman came to serve wine, while their coffee cooled in the cups in the morning parlor.

"You must have come running the minute you got my note," Norton said, smiling at this noble promptitude.

"Indeed, I did. I mentioned Papa was eager—"

"No excuses are necessary, laddie. We are delighted to see you anytime. And your friend, the duke, as well. When did you say he would be joining us?"

"I didn't! I have not heard from Crymont in weeks. I am pretty busy in the House." Norton frowned, and Havergal added, "At Westminster."

"Ah, that house. But surely you must bump into the duke there."

"No, Crymont takes little interest in politics."

"That may be, but no matter. He still takes an interest in pig racing, for as I was just telling Miss Lettie this very day, I saw his name in the paper in connection with those pig races in Green Park. He lost, I believe. Now when we get my Chester White bred with—"

"But it is not pig racing I have come to look into. It is pig *farming*." His eyes turned to Lettie in apology as he explained this. He found her examining him curiously. Their eyes held for a moment, as though judging each other anew.

"I made sure it was racing," Norton said. "Do you not think there's a pound to be made in it then?"

"A passing fancy, I fear. Next month it may be frogs or dogs or cats that catch on. Better stick to pork and bacon. I noticed as I came along that this is your hop farm, Mr. Norton. Where, exactly, is

128

your pig farm? I could run along there now and get out of your hair. I don't want to keep you from your work."

"Nonsense! Tomorrow is time enough for that. You won't want to hop back into your carriage so soon after a long trip. You will want to stretch your legs and have a bite to eat before dinner. Call for some tea, Miss Millie. I daresay Lord Havergal is famished."

The absurdity of having tea in preparation for dinner, while he held a glass of wine in his fingers, set Havergal's lips quivering. His eyes circled the room, looking for someone with whom to share this joke, and found Lettie chewing back a smile. Miss Milled called for tea, and the party resumed its chatter.

"I hope you aren't going to any special bother to entertain me," Havergal said earnestly, when three trays of sandwiches, cakes, and tea were brought in by a caravan of footmen. "It was presumptuous of me to invite myself, but I only meant it as a business meeting."

Norton smiled his reassurance. "No trouble at all. The ladies were coming to dinner this evening in any case, and they shall pick up the vicar and his wife along the way. The vicarage burned to the ground—poor souls. I invited them to stay here, but they are kin to half the village and have found rack and manger elsewhere."

"I am sorry to hear it. About the fire, I mean," Havergal said.

"The vicar goes to Canterbury on Thursday, Norton," his sister reminded him.

"So he does. Tomorrow evening then, Miss Millie. And this evening we shall just dine *en famille*, to let you rest up from your jaunt, Lord Havergal."

Havergal blinked to hear the ladies from Laurel Hall called family. Lettie disassociated herself from the whole thing by turning to exchange a few quiet words with Miss Millie. They were of a particularly harrowing nature on her hostess's part.

"What shall I serve him on such short notice!" Miss Millie asked, horrified. "And the new sheets not even put on the bed yet!"

"Just whatever you planned for yourselves," Lettie replied quietly.

"You and Miss Violet will come at least? Pray, do not abandon me, Miss Lettie. Do come, and we can have a hand of cards after, or Norton will prose His Lordship's ear off and make fools of us all."

Lettie found herself curiously eager to come. She noticed some new air about Havergal. Difficult to say just what it was, for he was quite as lively as before, yet more serious somehow. More eager to please. His eyes often turned to her in a searching way. As she recalled their last meeting, she thought perhaps he was just a little frightened of her. Was it for her benefit that he disclaimed any knowledge of Crymont and kept emphasizing that he was here for a serious study of hogs rather than for amusement?

"Yes, we shall come. As you are serving tea now, you won't want to serve dinner before seven or seven-thirty," she added, to avoid Miss Millie's rushing Havergal from tea table to dinner table.

"I doubt Cook can get things ready before seven. What will you wear? Do you think my diamonds and mauve lace gown will do?"

"Much too grand for a small dinner. Save them for the ball. I shall wear my bronze taffeta."

"Your blue crepe, Miss Millie," Violet suggested, "and that sapphire pendant on a gold chain that Norton bought you for your birthday."

"Oh I wish Norton would take His Lordship out, so that I could go and speak to Cook."

"Have your tea and then go ahead. Havergal will

not expect you to dance attendance on him when he has landed in on you unannounced. Just treat him like any ordinary guest."

Miss Millie looked at her as if she were mad. "By luck, I have a skinned hare hanging ready for the pan. That will prove some relief from pork and ham for tonight."

Domestic affairs of this sort made up the remainder of the ladies' teatime conversation. The banal nature of it left Lettie with one ear free to eavesdrop on the gentlemen. The talk was all of Berkshires and gilts and farrowing pens, which sounded as if Havergal was either actually here on business or putting on a good show. Time would tell.

She suggested that Miss Millie take advantage of their departure to exit herself from the room and attend to her duties, and leave the gentlemen to their business.

Havergal and Norton rose when the ladies began their departure.

"It was a pleasure to meet you again, ladies" was all Havergal said, but he said it with such a smile and with his eyes lingering just a second longer on Lettie than on Violet.

"You may want to just pick up your list of items for the public day, ladies," Norton said with a shrewd wink behind Havergal's back. "Anything you can think of to add will be entirely welcome."

They took this as a plea for input on the coming entertainments and took their papers home with them, smuggled out in their reticules.

"I am glad that is over with," Violet said when they were comfortably ensconced in Norton's carriage for the return trip. "I was dreading to meet Havergal again, but he doesn't appear to hold any grudge for the way you treated him."

"There was good cause for the way I treated him, Violet. And if you think the leopard has changed

131

his spots in a few short weeks, you are much mistaken." She said it as much to remind herself as to warn Violet, because whatever his spots, she still found him dangerously attractive.

Chapter Twelve

THERE FOLLOWED A week of entertainments unparalleled in the life of Ashford. The local worthies, eager to meet Miss Millie's noble guest, vied with one another in inventing amusements.

It was soon borne in on Lettie that, although she and Violet were included in most of the invitations, Lord Havergal had not been to call on them. Lettie was perfectly aware of the reason for it: she had told him bluntly on that awful night that he was never to set foot in her house again. As she sat down to dinner with him nearly every night in someone else's house, however, the interdict was beginning to look foolish. Sly hints from her friends let her know it was time she and Violet repay the neighbors' hospitality as well.

The highlight of the visit was to be Saturday, when the Nortons held their public day in the afternoon and their ball at night. Havergal had been talked into lengthening his visit to include these treats, but Lettie knew he would be leaving early in the next week. On Thursday, she and Violet were bidden to an alfresco party at Norton Knoll, and Lettie made a resolution that she would find an opportunity that very day to apologize to Havergal and give him permission to call. Surely her edict was all that was keeping him away. He was exceedingly friendly when they met and always went a little out of his way to distinguish her. If they chanced to meet on the street, he not only removed his hat and bowed, but stopped to chat for a few moments. If the assembly included dancing, he always stood up with her, usually first, and at Mrs. Pincombe's rout, first and last.

To dilute her triumph, Havergal had ridden out the next two afternoons with Miss Pincombe, whose papa kept the best stable in the neighborhood. Lord Havergal was known to be a bruising rider, and as he had come without mounts, it was settled among all the eligible ladies that he had to take Miss Pincombe's company to get his leg over Mr. Pincombe's bay mare.

During various conversations with Havergal, Lettie had come to realize that he was unaware of his father's visit to her. She felt odd not mentioning it, yet she had some vague feeling that Cauleigh did not wish it to be known. He had not enjoined her to secrecy, but he had not told his son of the call. She felt devious keeping it from him and determined to drop a casual mention of it the next time they had some privacy.

Lettie, along with most of the local ladies, had bought a new bonnet for this unprecedented Season of liveliness. It was a chip straw, particularly well suited to an alfresco party. She had not worn chip straw for five years, as it seemed to her a youthful fashion, yet as she tied the ribbons in front of the mirror, she thought it was not too youthful for her. Some new light had entered her eyes, some new happiness invaded her body, and it showed on her face. She looked younger. That was the closest she could come to putting words to it, and in her heart she knew Havergal was the cause.

Useless to say it was just the socializing, looking forward to Norton's ball, or even Tom's successful graduation, word of which had been received with much less excitement than it merited and would have received at any other time. The dreadful thought occurred to her that she looked like a lady in love. The only mitigation to her conscience was that every lady in town under the age of forty looked exactly the same way and for the same reason. Even Violet had blossomed into a new radiance and spoke casually of losing some weight as she peered in the mirror to view her new bonnet.

"You could stand to ease up on the sweets," Lettie allowed.

"Ned says I am just right!"

Mr. Norton had finally become Ned to them both. It seemed stiff to go on calling him Norton, or Mr. Norton, when Havergal had achieved a first-name basis inside of two days. Ned had slipped out unawares a few times, and Norton had seized eagerly on the chance to first-name the ladies as well. Indeed, Violet had already been shortened to Vi, and no doubt Lettie would have been further shortened to Let if it were not such an odd-sounding nickname.

The alfresco party was to commence at two-thirty in Norton's park, where a tent and serving table had been set up, with chairs ranged outside under the shelter of spreading elms. Musicians were hired, and for the unmusical a croquet field was available. Lettie was determined not to arrive gauchely early, but at two-fifteen she succumbed to Violet's entreaties and called the carriage. Arriving at two-forty, they found the whole polite village already there.

"So charming, quite a fête champêtre!" Violet exclaimed, smiling at the pretty bonnets and gowns and parasols, and the riot of brilliant blue tent brought for the occasion all the way from Canterbury. For no apparent reason a red and white awning also shaded the front door of the house.

As Lettie's practiced eye scanned the crowd for Havergal, she could find no unusual cluster of ladies, which usually served to locate him. Glancing at the awning, she saw him just issuing from it at a quick pace, adjusting his cravat as he came. No doubt Miss Millie's lunch had run late. He spotted her carriage and turned his footsteps toward it.

He politely aided the ladies' descent and unthinkingly tucked Lettie's fingers under his arm as they walked forward to join the party.

"I see Ned keeps you running, Havergal," Violet said. "Late for your own party."

"I feel as if I've fallen into the hands of a friendly sultan. I was never so regally entertained in my life. Most flattering," he said with one of his infamous smiles.

"Your harem awaits," Lettie said, as a group of ladies spotted him and came pelting forward, yelping like hounds on the scent of a fox.

His quick glance was apologetic and something more. Was it regret that darkened his gaze as he released her arm to make his bows?

"I've saved you a seat in the front row," Miss Pincombe told him, glancing to the chairs ranged in front of the raised stage.

"Was there not some talk of croquet?" he asked. "Such a fine day, it seems a shame to waste it sitting still for an hour."

Miss Palin elbowed her competitor aside and said, "We are just making up a team, Lord Havergal. You can partner me," and carried him off.

The concert was noticeably short of young female auditors. They were all, except Miss Beddoes and Miss Pincombe, out at the croquet field, disparaging Miss Palin's straw bonnet, gown, and handling of the mallet. Lettie began to see that a young gentleman's success might very well go to his head if he was similarly courted in London.

The general courting continued throughout the extravagant outdoor meal that followed the concert and croquet. It was beginning to seem that Lettie was not going to get her moment's privacy to apologize that day. When Miss Millie begged her to go into the house and just take a glance at the table for the ball, now only two days hence, Lettie was glad to escape the noise, sun, and sight of all the girls making cakes of themselves over Havergal.

They went to the dining room, where a shoeless footman was capering about on the spacious table that was spread with white linen. "Willie says the countess he last worked for always had him smooth the cloth this way," Miss Millie explained. "As we are dining out tonight and have no dinner parties planned till Saturday, we can use the breakfast parlor till then. I am getting a start on the dinner table for the ball today, for I shall be so busy getting ready for the public day tomorrow and then having it the day after, that there is no saying when it would get done if I left it. Now about that lobster casserole you gave me the receipt for, Lettie, tell me which plates to lay on for it. The red and gold rimmed ones seem the wrong size. I would not want things to look *odd*."

They discussed the table for ten minutes, at which time Miss Millie asked her friend's advice on the disposal of plants in the ballroom. "Just come along and see what I have done. Palms in all corners, and half a dozen lemon and orange trees from the orangery ranged along the side of the wall. I think the gardener must wail till tomorrow to arrange the cut blooms. They would never go two days without wilting, but I shall risk putting them out

Friday, for he will have his hands full Saturday at the public day. Norton put him in charge of the races."

"Where will you put the orchestra?" Lettie asked.

"There, at the far end, on that platform that is out in the park now," Miss Millie explained. "Ned plans to keep the awning up for the ball, but he will send back the tent tomorrow. The awning might come in handy if there is rain. The carriages could pull up right alongside it, and the ladies alight in the dryness. You don't think it *odd*?" she inquired. Lettie's thoughtless use of that adjective had stuck in Miss Millie's brain and was often referred to.

"Not in the least odd. That's a good idea, Miss Millie. Where will the flowers go?" Lettie inquired, looking all around. "The room looks huge without chairs, but when you've brought the chairs in from outside and ranged them around the room, there won't be much space for large vases of flowers."

"We must have flowers!"

"How about two large vases on pedestals on either side of the musicians' platforms?" Lettie suggested.

"What kind of pedestals?" Miss Millie asked anxiously.

"That set in Ned's study that hold the busts of Milton and Shakespeare would do nicely."

"Oh, you mean the statue stands. Yes indeed, an excellent idea. You know the answer to everything, Miss Lettie. I'll send for them at once to judge the effect."

She went into the hallway to summon a footman, and Lettie remained behind, looking around. Her imagination peopled the room with guests, music swirling through the air, and Havergal bending over her hand, asking her for a waltz. She drew a deep, luxurious sigh and turned to see Havergal

138

gazing at her. The room was empty again, stretching all around in awful silence, broken only by her unsteady breaths and the echo of her heartbeat in her ears.

He came forward, smiling. "So this is where you disappeared to."

"Oh," she exclaimed, flustered, "were you looking for me?"

"I wanted to apologize."

"For what?"

"For dashing off the moment you arrived."

"Ah, the crush of your harem," she said lightly.

"A new gent in town usually enjoys a week's favoritism, before the ladies realize he's just like all the other men," he said, shucking off his success.

"Your time is about up then."

"I have been hanging on unconscionably long, but Norton really is a mine of knowledge and so excessively hospitable that I am made to feel not only at home, but like a prodigal son."

"I'm sure he enjoys having you, but don't expect a fatted calf. It will be a suckling pig."

"I don't know how I shall ever repay him. Of course he will come to stay with Papa and me for a while when we begin setting up the operation and stocking our pens, but Papa leads a relatively retired life. This lavish way of entertaining would be too much for him."

"Blame it on Norton's enthusiasm," she said.

"It is not a question of blame! I hope you don't think I am complaining. Quite the contrary. Everyone has entertained me so generously—" He came to a conscious stop as it was borne in on them both simultaneously that hospitality had been withheld in one household. "Not that I mean—" Oh, Lord, that was only making it worse.

"I have been hoping for a moment to speak to you about that, Havergal," she said, trying for an air of ease she was far from enjoying. "I would like you to feel free to call at Laurel Hall anytime you are in the vicinity."

He looked at her uncertainly. "Are you sure?"

"Positive. Let us set an actual time, for a 'drop-in-any-time' invitation is no invitation at all. Come for tea tomorrow, you and the Nortons. Their servants will be busy preparing for the public day, and Miss Millie will be happy to dispense with preparing tea."

"Thank you, Miss Lettie. I shall be delighted. Of course I must check with my hostess first."

"Of course."

"Well, I am glad that is settled," he said with a happy smile. She could only conclude he was speaking of the invitation, as the acceptance was still in abeyance.

"I was a little harsh that night—" she said in some confusion.

"Indeed, you were not! You did exactly as you ought. It was unconscionable of me to—well, we both know what I did. No need to dredge up all that. I am quite a reformed character now, I promise you."

"I had a note from Crymont before he left. He generously took all the blame."

"*All* of it is doing it a bit brown. I should have made him send the girls back the minute I learned he had brought them. I should have written my apologies as well. Would you have read a note if I'd sent it?" he asked, and studied her face while she answered.

"Probably not. I daresay I would have fed it to the flames. I was out of reason cross with you and the duke." His perfectly natural way of speaking told Lettie that it was Crymont who had brought the girls, and without Havergal's knowledge. "He sounds like quite a rakehell," she said, shaking her head.

"So he is, and so was I, but I have changed my circle of friends and my behavior."

"That must be difficult."

"The most difficult thing was convincing Crymont I meant it. I tried to get him to give up that life of dissipation, but when he refused, I could do nothing. I have no authority over him. Ned tells me he is still racing pigs, and my own more intimate knowledge tells me he is doing a deal worse than that. Pity."

Lettie just smiled her approval, for she could suddenly think of no words to say. Some clogging of her throat would have made speech difficult in any case.

Seeing her mood, Havergal reached for her hand and began to lead her toward the doorway. Before they had gone two steps, he realized privacy was more likely in the ballroom and began touring it instead. "I think you know what has caused me to change the direction of my life?" he asked, peering down at her.

His glittering eyes suggested a very personal reason, one having to do with herself. Naturally, she feigned ignorance of his meaning. She said, "Was it the crush of debts, Havergal?"

"No, it was the lecture those debts precipitated in a certain quarter."

"It was not your trying to cadge money from the trust that precipitated my lecture, sir!" she reminded him, but playfully.

"Indirectly it was. I would not have been at Laurel Hall otherwise. If I had not needed the money so desperately, I would not have made such a barnacle of myself, when you obviously wished me at Jericho! The lack of warmth in that invitation to dinner!"

"It was wash day. We were planning to dine on cold ham and bread pudding. Not a meal to ask a man to, as Doctor Johnson would say."

"Strangely I have no recollection at all of what we actually ate," he said, frowning at this oddity.

"Not even the overdone potatoes that were discussed to death?" she laughed. It seemed incredible that that evening could now elicit amusement.

"Ah, the potatoes. And Miss Beddoes prohibiting us from further discussion of them, but not suggesting any alternative subject! I was beginning to feel we were at a cloistered monastery where speaking was not permitted. And then when Crymont landed in and later lured me to the inn—" He shook his head ruefully. "I decided that scrambling out of windows and lying to my hostess was conduct unworthy of a Cauleigh. I have been wanting to explain it to you for a long time. Now I find that the explanation shows me in a wretched light as well, for the second evening I knew the girls were there."

"You mean you paid *two* visits to the inn!" she exclaimed.

"The first evening I didn't know the girls were there. I thought it was only for dinner and wine. *Now* your dinner is coming back to me!" he laughed. "At least I remember it was inadequate, for I was looking forward with pleasure to that baron of beef Crymont mentioned. As soon as I learned of the women, I left. I didn't even see them that night."

"Was it curiosity that drew you back the second evening, then?"

"I cannot claim that excuse. We met them in the village, if you recall. The less said of that contretemps, the better. And I, like a ninnyhammer, pulled the reins instead of bolting past. No, it was threats that drew me back the second evening.

Cherry Devereau has the devil's own temper. Crymont convinced me she would create havoc if I didn't go. So she would, too," he said with no air of rancor. "But at least I did not give your servants the wine. Crymont left it in the stable. On his behalf I should explain that he never thought it would all be consumed in one night."

"It is just as well you broke off with Crymont" is all she said. Havergal's past was obviously scarlet, but a scarlet past will often cast a rosy glow on those who have had the fortitude to abandon it. She sensed an air of glamour, almost of the hero, about Havergal. His war had been not with the French or even a neighbor, but with his own character, and he had triumphed. He had left behind that life of dissolution, and he imagined that she had something to do with his victory.

"There is one thing that surprised me, Miss Lettie," he said with a quizzing smile. "Why did you agree to continue administering my trust? I made sure I had lost all contact with you when Papa told me of your decision to abandon it."

"Your father asked me to reconsider. He called at Laurel Hall to do so. I did it to please him, really." She listened with curiosity to hear what he had to say of that visit.

"Now there is a facer for me. I had some hope that you had learned of my new and improved character. The journals have quite given up on me. I haven't been done since I sold my hunters to pay off that thousand pounds. I was shown with tears in my eyes on that occasion, crying while Alvanley led Thor and Zeus away. I did feel close to tears, too."

She was surprised that he paid so little heed to hearing that his father had called on her. Havergal assumed his papa had been in the neighborhood and paid a courtesy call, mentioning the trust in passing.

A commotion at the doorway proved to be Miss Millie, leading two stout footmen, each carrying a pedestal. The private moment was over, but Lettie took advantage of the interruption to ask Millie to bring Havergal to Laurel Hall for tea the next afternoon. Miss Millie said she must check with Ned, and meanwhile would Lettie and Havergal just advise her on the disposition of the pedestals. As this job was going forth, Mr. Norton joined them.

"So here you are, laddie! All the ladies are pawing the ground with eagerness to get at you. Best foot it quickly. They are threatening to set up a revolution outside." He took hold of Havergal's elbow to lead him out.

"Before you go, Ned," his sister said, "are we free for tea at Laurel Hall tomorrow? Miss Lettie has invited us."

"I fear not. There are a hundred things to do to get the public day set up. Why don't you and Vi join us here, Lettie? More hands, less work. You ladies can wrap up the prizes and oversee the servants."

This left no possibility of repaying hospitable debts, but it ensured being with Havergal, and Lettie accepted. "Another time, then. Perhaps dinner on Sunday. Are you free then?" she asked.

"Check the schedule, Miss Millie," Norton said, and finally led his guest away.

"Sunday is fine," Miss Millie said, and it was settled.

In the park, Havergal found himself being jostled mercilessly by the ladies. Such a lack of pride in their fawning over him, actually grabbing at his coat sleeve and thrusting their faces into his, like demanding puppies. He thought of Lettie's calm behavior and felt its attraction more keenly. She was looking lovely today. She seemed younger, prettier, every time he met her. In fact, she seemed the sort of lady who grew more desirable on a longer acquaintance. He must watch his step, or he'd go tumbling into love with her.

When the ladies returned to Laurel Hall, Lettie found she had only the vaguest memories of the remainder of that afternoon. It was as though her spool of memory stopped in the ballroom, when Havergal looked deeply into her eyes and said, "I think you know what has caused me to change the direction of my life?"

She felt, in some disturbing way, that that moment had changed the direction of hers.

Chapter Thirteen

IT WAS HALF a relief to awaken in the morning to leaden skies and a mist of rain. Lettie was not optimistic enough to expect three days of sun in a row, and today's rain held out some hope for sunny skies for Norton's public day on Saturday. She and Violet spent the morning planning their Sunday dinner, with particular care to the guest list.

Cook was called to the saloon to discuss a menu. To outdo Norton's opulent hospitality was impossible, but Lettie intended to atone for that bread pudding and ordered the best meal Mrs. Siddons could handle. As Havergal had casually mentioned looking forward to a baron of beef at the Royal Oak, Lettie insisted on a roast of beef. With more pork than she knew what to do with in her larder, she also asked for a platter of cutlets, as a change from roast meat. They discussed fish, fowl, vegetables, and dessert for an hour.

"I'd best get busy then" was Mrs. Siddons comment when they were finished, "for it will take two days to cook up all this mess of pottage."

"We shall be out for tea, and an omelet will do for our dinner," Lettie said, to cajole her.

"Omelet, is it, and me with a ten-pound pork joint already roasted."

"Cold pork for sandwiches then," Lettie decided.

The rain had still not let up by lunch, but it had not worsened either. "It is one of those *horrid* days when it is going to drizzle from dawn to dusk," Violet said. "We shall have to spend the entire day inside."

Lettie refused to be downcast. "Where else would we wrap presents?" The inclement weather made it more likely that Havergal would be confined within doors as well.

He was, for all the good it did her. He was kept busy in Norton's study, drawing up a model pig barn to be run upon scientific lines. Until teatime he might as well not have been in the house at all, but at four o'clock Norton released him and brought him to the table.

The talk was all of pig business, and while Lettie did not particularly enjoy or even understand it, she was aware of a new sense of purpose about Havergal. He spoke knowledgeably about the business. She was content with such crumbs as fell her way. Long glances while Norton talked, fleeting smiles when he managed to overhear some remark she made to Miss Millie, and a general air of what she could only call consciousness. She felt in her bones that he was acutely conscious of her close presence, as she was conscious of his.

After tea, he suggested escorting her to the ballroom to see the final disposition of the flowers. The ruse was spoiled by Miss Millie's accompanying them, but Lettie appreciated the effort. A tray of dance cards stood ready at the entrance. Norton succumbed to extravagance and had them edged in gilt, with gold satin tassels. As they were leaving, they let Miss Millie go on ahead of them. Havergal selected a card, wrote his name in for the first dance, and handed it to Lettie, peering to see if she approved.

"That is to ensure that you come early," he said.

"You wish to get your duty over and done with, that you might enjoy the remainder of the evening," she answered coquettishly.

His gaze lingered on that flirtatious smile. "On the contrary." He took the card back and wrote again. When he handed it back, she saw he had also filled in the last dance. "That ensures that you remain till the end—and that I have something to look forward to."

"Two dances! That will occasion gossip, sir!"

"I have no doubt your redoubtable reputation can withstand it. Mine, of course, is more fragile."

"My advanced years must be my protection."

"Not for a decade, Lettie. You wear them too lightly. You will do the right thing by me and marry me if I become an object of censure, I trust?"

She read laughter in his bottomless eyes, but it was shared laughter. She was thrilled at the suggestion of a betrothal, even in this frivolous way. And as they stood together, the laughter faded, and she watched, entranced, as his expression changed to a more sober sort of anticipation. "Lettie!" He grabbed her hands and looked around, to be sure they were alone.

"It would be improper for a guardian to marry her charge, would it not?" she parried. Her voice came out light and strained.

"Highly improper and just what you might expect of the horrid Lord Havergal," he said. His voice was an intimate whisper. He pulled her closer to him. His arms went around her, his face drew closer till his handsome features were a blur, then his lips touched hers lightly, in an exploratory way. They felt cool, perhaps because her own were fevered. Lettie felt the room begin to spin. She closed her eyes and became aware of the scent of flowers and the spice aroma from the orange and lemon trees. It all seemed unreal, especially his arms crushing her against the hard wall of his chest. It was surely a dream.

As suddenly as he had kissed her, he released her. "You'll have to attack Papa again about being rid of that trust," he said. How could he find breath to speak after that kiss? Lettie just gazed, unhearing.

They continued back to the tearoom. Lettie felt she was floating on clouds.

Norton glanced out the window and said, "I hope you won't take the idea I am trying to be rid of you, but you might be wise to seize this minute of letup in the drizzle to get home, Vi."

Lettie felt something jarring in his speech. She soon figured out what it was. That remark ought to have ended in Miss Lettie or, under the new regime, Lettie. But it was at Violet that he was smiling in his open, approving manner. When had this happened? Violet was simpering in a way that hinted at dalliance while the others were out of the room.

Lettie was deeply disturbed by her own dalliance, but she pushed it to the back of her mind for reliving in private later and teased her friend on the journey home. "You are quite usurping my place in Ned's affections, Violet."

Violet blushed up to the roots of her hair and said, "What nonsense! I'm sure he would have you if you so much as nodded at the man. I cannot imagine why you do not, Lettie. Really he is so good-humored and not at all bad-looking."

"And rich," Lettie added. "This match has my blessing."

"It is not a match! How can you say so!"

The more she denied it, the redder she blushed,

149

and the more likely it seemed that a match was brewing. Lettie's mind was preoccupied with her own musings, and Violet seemed content to continue the drive in silence.

When they met for dinner, Lettie said, "Did Ned happen to mention where they are exhibiting Havergal this evening?"

"You make him sound like a wild beast! They are dining at Pincombes'. A small party, consisting of only themselves, to give Miss Pincombe unhampered access to Havergal. So obvious! She is chasing him as hard as she can. Miss Millie said they shan't stay late, for she has her hands full at this time."

It annoyed Lettie that Havergal would be spending the evening with Miss Pincombe. She was a pretty girl, well dowered, but in local opinion considered too forthcoming. A touch of brass would not bother Havergal. On her dresser there sat no dance card with his name inscribed for the first and last dances. He had not kissed her. That was her consolation. He *hadn't* kissed Miss Pincombe, had he?

Lettie planned an early evening to brace herself for the strenuous day and evening awaiting them on the morrow. At nine o'clock she said, "I'm going upstairs now, Violet. I'm going to do my hair up in papers. Make sure Siddons locks up."

"You cannot go yet!" Violet exclaimed in agitation. Lettie looked a question, and she continued. "Ned mentioned he might drop in after dinner. Miss Millie has to dash home, but Havergal was to take his own carriage, and he can deliver her home. Ned is going to drop off a book for me."

Lettie gave her a sapient smile. "I didn't know he had one. What is this important book?"

"There is no need to be satirical, Lettie. Ned often reads. It happens to be a copy of Miss Edgeworth's *Castle Rackrent*."

"I see. Then in that case, I must remain below-stairs to play propriety. Shall I play it from the study, or will you two require closer guardian-ship?"

"You must stay in the saloon, Lettie. It is a social call, no more."

It occurred to Lettie that there was no impropri-ety in Miss Millie being taken home by the groom, leaving Havergal free to join Norton in the delivery of the book. With this in mind she dashed upstairs and attended to her toilette. She was nonchalantly thumbing through a fashion magazine, with her new shawl protecting her shoulders and a fresh rib-bon in her curls, when the awaited knock came. She looked eagerly to the doorway and felt her heart bound with joy. He had come!

Norton had soon ensconced himself on the sofa by the fire with Violet, narrating in detail the story of the drunken Sir Patrick and his cohorts in ad-venture. "A dandy story, though I was a little dis-appointed that Sir Condy Rackrent upped and died in the end, without marrying his Judy. It was the drink did him in. Here, I'll just read you the ending of it. Have your hankie at the ready, Vi, for it will bring forth a tear from such a softhearted lady as yourself."

After hearing a prolonged relating of the gist of the book, it seemed hard to now have to hear it read. "Would you mind if I visit your library, Miss Lettie?" Havergal asked. "Hearing that excellent recital makes me hungry for more of Miss Edge-worth.

"I have a copy of *Belinda* somewhere," she re-plied, and jumped up with alacrity to accompany him.

The library was in darkness, and Havergal helped her light lamps all around. "Miss Violet is magnanimous, not to beat him over the head with the book when he told her the ending," he mentioned. She watched as the candle flame caught and played over his face. The moving light flickered on his clean-cut jaw, the handsome nose, and well-carved lips. His lips opened, and a flash of white teeth showed in a disturbing smile.

"I believe the book was only a ruse," she said.

"Is there a match brewing between them?"

"It begins to look that way."

Without so much as glancing at the bookshelves, they sat in front of the cold grate and began talking. "That will leave you alone here. What word is there of Tom? You have not forgotten you are to send him to me when he goes to London?"

"He has graduated. He will be in London next week, but as you will be at Willow Hall ..." She waited on nettles to hear what he might say. A gentleman did not kiss a lady unless he planned to propose very shortly.

"I am back and forth frequently. I am on the committee to study grain tariffs, and am often in the House. Actually, my new activities put me in closer touch with gentlemen who can assist him. An unlooked-for perk in my new life of rectitude."

"I shall write him this very evening," she said, pleased at the offer and blushing to think of past missives, telling Tom that he was in no circumstance to have anything to do with Havergal, though the Duke of Crymont's help was still allowed. She must inform Tom otherwise when she wrote.

A moment later it had been tacitly established that they would wait out the entire visit in the library. "That cold grate is inhospitable," Lettie said. "Let us have it lit and call for wine."

"The fire is already laid. No need to wait for a servant to light it. I'll do it while you send for the wine."

While he busied himself with the tinderbox, Lettie asked for wine and biscuits. Soon they were enjoying a friendly blaze and a glass of sherry.

"Perhaps you would have preferred claret," she said.

"It is not the wine that matters to me, but the company. I little thought we would ever become so—friendly, Lettie. May I drop the 'miss' now that we are friends?" She nodded her acquiescence. "My name is Jacob," he said. "The family calls me so. I would be happy if you would, too."

This set her quite apart from Miss Pincombe, and she felt great pleasure in his request. "I noticed your father called you that."

"Odd that Papa called on you."

"Yes, I was surprised."

"I expect he was in the neighborhood. I hope he didn't give you a wretched reading of my character. He is vastly impressed with my transformation. In fact, he has turned five thousand pounds over to me without my even asking, to invest in that new printing press I discussed with you on a former occasion. I was greatly touched, more at the show of trust than the money, though I do think it an excellent investment."

"If you continue on this new path, your hunting lodge in the Cotswolds may see its new coat of paint yet."

He turned a luminous smile on her. "Anything seems possible." He gazed a long time into her eyes and repeated, "Anything," in a low, deep voice that sent a quiver up her spine. Surely his glowing eyes suggested the most impossible "anything" of all, that he loved her. "What will you do when Violet leaves you, Lettie?" he asked.

Her heart plunged. "A match is by no means certain. We have not discussed that possibility at all."

"They smell of April and May to me. If it comes

to a match—you will not want to stay on here alone."

"No, I don't think I would like that. I'll have to invite someone to accompany me."

He rubbed his chin pensively. "You won't be doing anything immediately, I take it?"

"Not unless and until Violet accepts an offer from Norton."

He nodded, satisfied with her answer. He wondered why his father had visited Miss Beddoes, and why he hadn't mentioned it. He would not make an offer without discussing it with Papa, especially when he had just regained his father's confidence. He felt that more time was required to ingratiate the lady as well. A kiss did not loom so large in his mind as in Lettie's. First help Tom to a good position; that would soften her up. Continuing to see her posed a problem, however. He could not hang on at Norton Knoll forever, and to invite her to Willow Hall was tantamount to an offer. London occurred to him as a possibility.

"Did you ever think of taking up residence with Tom in London?" he mentioned.

"No, someone must be here to look after things."

"A visit to London, to see Tom settled in, then?"

"I am not at all imaginative, Havergal." He gave her a look, not angry, but not happy either. "That never occurred to me. Tom is grown now. He can arrange his own accommodations."

"I think you would enjoy London. There is so much to do—balls and concerts and plays."

"All those delights that led you astray," she teased.

"You are made of stronger stuff," he said approvingly. "Virtue should be rewarded. I still enjoy balls and plays—and your excellent sherry." He held his glass out in a toast. "I have not turned into a Methodist, Lettie. Nor have I turned into Jacob," he reminded her. Was that why he had given that strange look? She had inadvertently called him Havergal, as she was in the habit of doing. "What I require is a coat of many colors, to remind you who I am."

Her lips moved unsteadily. "I believe that was Joseph, Havergal."

He grimaced. "That was an unnecessary display of ignorance on my part."

"Jacob, if memory serves, was the clever gent who bought his brother Esau's birthright for a mess of pottage."

"I wonder Papa didn't christen me Esau; that sounds more in my improvident style."

"Your *old* style, that is."

"Quite so. You have changed me beyond all recognition. At the risk of boring you, I shall repeat, I never dared to hope you and I would be so comfortable together, sitting by the fireside like Darby and Joan, discussing the *Bible*."

A smile quivered across her lips. "That seems a strange and modest thing to hope for, Jacob."

He reached out and touched her cheek. "There, that wasn't so hard to say, was it, Lettie?" His finger lingered, falling in a slow caress as he gazed at her.

No, she wasn't imagining it. If Havergal had indeed reformed, he would not flirt so outrageously with a respectable lady. He was working up to an offer.

"I have no problem with Jacob," she allowed in a strained voice. "It is the Ezekiel's and Zedekiah and Mahalaheel's that confuse me."

"Good. I wouldn't want you to be confused about *me*."

The talk turned to less emotionally charged subjects: the public day, the ball, and the local society. After half an hour they rejoined Ned and Violet.

They were met with no firm announcement, but after the gentlemen left, Violet said, "Are you quite sure you have no interest in Ned, Lettie?"

"I have a keen interest in him, for he would make you a charming husband. I hope you will invite me to your wedding."

"He hasn't asked me yet. I mean he hasn't asked me," she said, and held *Castle Rackrent* to her heart, as though it were made of gold.

Such an odd book to be forever enshrined in Violet's mind with romance, Lettie thought. Yes indeed, anything seemed possible, since Havergal's coming to town.

Chapter Fourteen

A MAN'S FIRST idea of heaven is implanted early in his youth. For Mr. Norton, the idea had not changed much since the forty or so years ago when he had first heard of it at his mother's knee. He still envisaged it as rather a dull place, with saints and angels sitting on clouds, playing harps. On that Saturday in May when his public day was held, he was struck with the original thought that everyone's heaven could be different. It could be an infinite continuation of the best day of one's life, and for Mr. Norton it would unquestionably be one endless public day, with himself the host, and the entire neighborhood, not only the commoners but the gentry, bowing, smiling, and congratulating him.

The shouting and squealing of kiddies running and dogs barking, and both destroying his parkland, sent quivers of joy through his body. "Mr. Norton" seemed to hang on every lip. At the end of each contest, there was a prize to be meted out by himself, followed by a round of applause. When he tired of this, he could stand behind the main refreshment table in his new cinnamon jacket, personally distributing glasses of wine, lemonade, ratafia, or orgeat to the ladies. Particular friends received a knowing nod and wink, and a whispered word, "You won't want to bother with this slop, Miss Pincombe. There is champagne in the tent." There was a burly footman in a new suit of livery guarding the tent entrance, to see that commoners did not sneak in and enjoy this privileged treat.

He smiled benignly on Miss FitzSimmons, who accompanied him on his rounds, praising everything and smoothing the course of conversation with the more elevated guests. He kept Lord Havergal in his eye and noticed that he was often with Lettie. It would remove the last block from his path if he could convince the lad to offer for Lettie. It seemed a shabby trick to dump her for Vi, but if she could nab another fellow, he need have no scruples about offering for her companion.

Busy as his eyes and mind were kept with all this, he often spared a glance toward the road, to see if a certain carriage with strawberry leaves on the door appeared. Crymont had not replied to his invitation, which looked as if he had not received it. On the other hand, the duke might pop in at the last minute to add the coup de grace to this exquisite day. He knew from Havergal that the two lads had had a falling out. What pleasure it would give him to bring about a reconciliation under his roof. Duke and viscount, one day to be an earl, both sitting at his table. The only possible addition to his glory would be to see the duke offer for Miss Millie, but even his optimism did not soar to such heights as this. Even heaven must have some limitation.

Lettie enjoyed the afternoon, too, and would have enjoyed it even more if there had been no one there but herself and Havergal. His duties as vice-host kept him from her at times, but he returned often and co-opted her help in his duties, too. Together they bound up the children's ankles for the three-legged race, handed out eggs and spoons for the egg race, and put bags over children's heads for the blindman's race. Havergal was helpful in keeping the dogs from joining the races and comforting the losers. Lettie watched, pleased to see him making himself useful—doing it all with no air of condescension, but truly taking pleasure from such humble pursuits.

"I think you have done this sort of thing before, Jacob," she smiled.

"I am an old hand at public days. I must be getting home for our own. Papa holds it in June. Have you given any thought to going to London, to visit Tom?"

"No," she said, gazing across the field to where Violet and Norton were holding court. "But if Violet accepts an offer, I daresay she will want to go to London to prepare her trousseau, and I would go with her."

"Drop me a line at Willow Hall when you are going, and I'll make a point to be there. And before you object to writing to a bachelor, let me remind you, you are also my guardian."

"The visit is by no means certain," she pointed out, and waited to hear what else he might suggest.

He just smiled confidently. "I'll put a bee in Ned's bonnet, and you do the same with Miss Vi. Between us, we'll get them to the altar—and you to London."

Havergal was called away to judge the singing contest, and Lettie went to sit in the audience and ponder his harping on London. Was it eagerness to see her again that prompted it? She didn't know how else they should meet, unless he invited her to Willow Hall—and that would be as good as an offer. Did he think Lord Cauleigh would not approve? Was that why Jacob had not come to the sticking point? Papa liked her well enough as a guardian, but no doubt he was looking higher for the future Lady Havergal. If there was opposition in that quarter, clandestine meetings in London would hardly assist the case. Surely Havergal was aware of that. There was really no point in meeting him in London at all. He either cared for her, or he didn't. If he did, then he must confront his father with the fact and invite her home. And if he had nothing in mind but a flirtation, then he may go to the devil.

Her mood was uncertain as she prepared for the ball that evening. Excitement and anticipation were paramount, but at the bottom of her heart there rested a corner of doubt. Havergal seemed a different man from the one who had first come storming into her saloon, demanding to see Mr. Beddoes, but in reality, only a month had passed. Was it possible for a man to change so much in so short a time?

She studied him during dinner at Norton Knoll, a grand meal with twenty-four at the table. He sat across from her and looked so handsome, she felt a pang of jealousy every time he spoke to his partners. An exuberant bouquet of flowers impeded her vision. Only the top half of his face was visible above a cluster of roses, but by inclining rather far to the right, she could see his whole face.

Dinner was a splendid affair, with enough courses and removes to rival the banquets at the prince's Brighton Pavilion. When the ladies retired to the saloon to allow the gentlemen leisure for port and blowing a cloud, Miss Millie came tripping over to Lettie and Violet.

"I have never seen Norton happier," she said, and sat down with a sigh of relief that her chief duties were over for the evening.

"What a banquet!" Violet exclaimed. "I don't know how I am to lose any weight with such feasting as this, Miss Millie."

"Why, you will dance it all off before the night is

over. Norton tells me Lord Havergal and I are to lead off, as he is the guest of honor and I am the hostess. I will be the envy of all the young ladies. Quite a star in my crown."

Lettie stared in consternation. "I thought Norton and Violet would lead off!" she exclaimed.

"Oh no. Norton wishes Havergal to start the dancing, because of the title, you know. The highest title is given that honor, or so Norton says. He has his heart quite set on it. We would not want to end up the evening in an odd way."

"Of course," Lettie said, trying to quell her disappointment. She would have the second dance with Havergal—and the last. But she had been looking forward to that first one.

The gentlemen did not tarry long over their port. Norton was eager to see his full party rejoined, and Havergal did nothing to delay the proceedings. As they left the room, Norton said, "I trust you have your dancing slippers oiled, laddie. Miss Millie has spoken of nothing but the honor of opening the ball with you."

"But I—of course, Ned. I am looking forward to it."

He made a beeline for Lettie as soon as he entered the saloon. Norton was close behind him, and soon the host's raucous company had the other ladies occupied.

Havergal said quietly to Lettie, "Something has come up, Lettie. About our first dance—"

"I know," she said, making a moue. "I have been relegated to second place behind Miss Millie."

Havergal smiled at that moue, so attractive, and so unlike the Miss Beddoes he had first known. Lettie had blossomed into a flirt before his very eyes. The smile faded as he considered what he had to tell her. He tried to make a joke of it, but in truth he was unhappy and frustrated.

"Worse, dear heart. As the beau of the ball, my card is full. That is to say, I have been signed up for all the other dances."

"But the dance cards haven't even been issued yet!"

"What a slow top you are, Lettie!" he teased. "All the dashers sneaked a card this afternoon and have been circulating them clandestinely. Miss Pincombe has suborned me for the second set, Miss Seton for the third, and some girl in a yellow gown has got me for the fourth. Unless we can arrange to break someone's leg, we are not going to have our dance till the end of the evening. Are you as disappointed as I am?"

"I shall be graceful in defeat and say it doesn't matter in the least."

"I don't call that graceful! *I* am *devastated*. You might at least allow you are disappointed."

"Very well then, I am disappointed."

"There is always supper," he said, to console her. "I lied and told all my harem, as you call them, that I already had a partner for that. Presumptuous of me. Perhaps you have made other plans?"

"No, I am not so perspicacious as the other ladies, it seems. I neither filled my card nor arranged a supper partner before the ball even began. I am such a laggard, I don't put on my bonnet till I am ready to go out."

"I daresay you wouldn't say yes till a gentleman asked you either," he said with a daring smile.

"Perhaps not even then. I might say no instead, depending on the gentleman and, of course, the question."

His brows rose in surprise. "One assumes that the question is of a purely legitimate nature. I cannot imagine anyone brave enough to confront Miss Beddoes with any other sort."

"Assuming the question is unexceptionable, there

remains only the matter of the gentleman's identity."

He took her fan and examined it. Then he peered up and said, "I think we both know what gentleman we are speaking of."

Lettie felt a heat invade her body. Her throat was dry, and she said, feeling foolish, "You know my method now, Havergal."

"Jacob!"

"Jacob. When I hear a question, then I shall give an answer."

He gazed into her eyes a long moment, while the world seemed to hold its breath. "I give you fair warning, Lettie, that will be very soon. Prepare your reply."

She was fully prepared to give it that very moment. Before more was said, however, there was a commotion amidst the chairs beside them, and Mr. Norton stood up. "I hear the squawk of the fiddles coming from the ballroom. Are you and Miss Millie set to stand up and jig it, laddie?"

"Ready and waiting," Havergal replied, and rose to offer Miss Millie his arm. He said aside to Lettie as he left, "Better hop to it and get a new name on that card, or you'll be propping up the wall for the next half hour."

In fact, Lettie had no difficulty filling her card. There were men enough to go around, and as she had no interest in whether or not the gentlemen were married, eligible, handsome, or ugly as sin, she accepted the first ones who offered. It was all just filling time till supper, and after that it would be more waiting for the last dance. She enjoyed comparing the ladies' toilettes, watching Violet and Ned getting on so well, and in general seeing her friends. It was a grand version of the local assemblies, only better, because she caught an occasional

163

glimpse of Havergal through the throng and knew that he loved her. At least it seemed wonderfully like love.

Chapter Fifteen

At last midnight came, and the crowd began leaving the ballroom for the supper parlor. She saw Havergal looking all around with an eager face. When he spotted her, his smile beamed, and he hurried forward. The party was to be seated at a series of small tables, with Norton and his group of twelve, which included the ladies from Laurel Hall, at the head of the room. Havergal tucked Lettie's hand under his arm, and they went toward the parlor.

Norton was at the doorway, a smile splitting his happy face. "I have a surprise for you, laddie," he said archly. "You will never guess who has landed in on us. He is waiting at the table. I had to squeeze him in between you and Lettie, but you shan't mind when you see who it is. Mind you, it is not only you he has come to see. It is my swinery that is half the attraction, I fancy. That is what has lured him hither."

"Ah, I wrote him about the swinery. So he has come to see it for himself. I am delighted!" Havergal replied.

He gave an expectant smile. Papa! he thought. Excellent. It will give him an opportunity to know

Lettie a little better. We can sweep her up and take her home with us. He hurried forward, taking Lettie with him. Lettie read his pleasure and excitement, but had no idea who the unexpected guest could be.

Havergal looked to the table and saw Crymont. The duke was outfitted in a ridiculous jacket of white satin, heavily embroidered in gold threads. He held a quizzing glass aloft, scanning the throng for pretty girls. Havergal's heart sank like a stone in water. Good God! What was *he* doing here? He looked to Norton, who still smiled benignly. "What do you think of this, eh?"

The man thought he was bestowing a marvelous treat, but Havergal would rather have seen the devil himself than Crymont. The awful idea darted into his head that there were more lightskirts at the inn, ready to cause havoc. He'd have to get Crymont alone and question him. God only knew what trouble Norton had gone to to arrange this visit, and he must simulate some sign of pleasure.

"What a delightful surprise," he said weakly, and went forward, smiling, to shake Crymont's hand. They stood a little off from the table. In his perturbed state, Havergal didn't notice that Lettie had withdrawn her hand and fallen behind.

She went reluctantly to her chair between the gentlemen, looking about for someone to change seats with, but the ladies were all beginning to sit down at their allotted spots. Impossible to ask Violet to change seats with her. She would want to sit by Norton. Perhaps Miss Millie ... She hastened to her side and said, "As the hostess, you should sit beside the duke, Miss Millie."

"Should I? Oh dear! How shall we arrange it? The table is so odd, with an extra chair squeezed in."

"Change seats with me," Lettie said, and it was

done. She took up Miss Millie's seat beside the vicar, listening as Havergal greeted his old friend.

"I am surprised to see you here, Crymont."

"I caved in to repeated urgings, dear boy. It was not the hope of buying a good racing pig that convinced me, but a desire to see you again. I cannot like to see you turning into a country bumpkin. I have come to rescue you."

"Come and make your bows to the ladies," Havergal said, to detour this line of talk.

Crymont came strolling forward and made an exquisite bow to the table before taking his seat. Lettie nodded coolly and immediately lifted her wineglass to obviate any further greeting.

Havergal noticed her removal and was grateful for it. There was no saying what might come out of Crymont's mouth, as he had been drinking more than a little. Havergal recognized the signs: a certain flush in the cheeks, an exaggeration in the drawling speech, and a heaviness about the eyelids.

The table was buzzing with conversation. Lettie pecked at her food and tried to hear, above or below the general roar, what was passing between Crymont and Havergal. She caught only discrete phrases, but as she tried to put them into some meaning, she disliked what she was hearing. Crymont congratulated Havergal for having "got five thousand out of the old man. That will more than replenish your team." That would be the five thousand ostensibly invested in the new printing press. She noticed Havergal replied in low, inaudible tones, discerned his nervous mood, and suspected the worst. She noticed, too, that he frequently cast guilty glances in her direction.

"A marvelous party," Crymont said later. "Iona was asking for you. I told her . . ." Norton's hearty laughter boomed out, covering the rest of it. She saw Havergal incline his head to Crymont in eager speech.

"For God's sake, don't mention that woman's name here," Havergal cautioned. "I trust you are traveling alone this time. No surprises waiting for me at the inn."

"Just one little surprise—and no happy one, I fear. I am in the suds, Havergal. Can't pay my reckoning at the inn. I was wiped out at the South-ampton races. Bingo Compton is with me, waiting for his blunt. Can you let me have two hundred?"

"I don't have that much cash on me. I can give you ten."

"That won't begin to cover it. I owe Bingo one fifty, and shall need some money to get to London."

"Write the innkeeper a check."

"He refused to cash a check for me. If you're caught short yourself, come along and vouch for me. I expect they know you at the inn by now. I do have the money in the bank. It is not as though I planned to rob the knave."

"Very well, but it will have to wait till after the ball."

"But of course! I plan to dance till dawn. I see 'Mr.' Beddoes, the Turk, is glowering at you, as usual."

Havergal looked along the board and saw the same thing. He felt a helpless sense of frustration, but he lifted his glass in a salute and drank. Lettie acknowledged it with a nod, but she didn't raise her glass or even smile.

Crymont observed the pass and gave Havergal a jeering look. "It must be demmed awkward, having to meet her socially, after the way she treated you last time. The woman is a yahoo."

"I happen to value Miss Beddoes's good opinion."

"In that case, I shall do my poor best to conciliate her."

"I would prefer that you not do that, Crymont."

"Don't be a bore, Havergal. She is turning you into a prig. Next you'll be prating of ethics. Do come back to London with me. Iona would be happy, and so would I."

The dinner was finally over, and the crowd returned to the ballroom. Lettie was much of a mind to leave, but as Violet was determined to stay till the end, she capitulated and contented herself with being cool to Crymont and Havergal. They did not speak to her, for the very good reason that Havergal took pains to keep them apart, finding other partners to keep the duke occupied. Much depended on the last dance.

Eventually the moment arrived, and Havergal was bowing before her, all his charm intact, and doing much to soften her ire. "I didn't know he was coming" were the first words he said. "I had no idea. He tells me Norton wrote to him, believing it was a special treat for me. That is why I had to pretend I was pleased."

"Is the duke traveling alone?" she inquired.

"With a friend—a gentleman," he said with a look that both acknowledged and answered her real question. "They will be proceeding directly to London."

"Traveling on Sunday. What more could one expect?" she sniffed.

Havergal looked at her, surprised. "The ban on unnecessary Sunday traveling is falling into limbo. It is only provincials and religious fanatics who cling to it," he said. The words were out before he realized he had caused offense.

"When in the provinces, one ought to do as the provincials do," she retorted.

They were saved by the scraping of the bow and went to join a set. The ball closed with a rowdy country dance that gave no privacy and very little pleasure. As he led Lettie from the floor, Havergal said, "May I call on you tomorrow? I plan to leave on Monday. No desecrating the Sabbath for me," he added, to show there were no hard feelings on that score.

"You are to come to dinner tomorrow, Havergal. Have you forgotten? You cannot be looking forward to it with as much pleasure as I."

"I remembered! But the house will be full of guests. We will have no privacy. As I shall be leaving so soon, could I not come in the afternoon as well?"

Lettie was planning a more elaborate dinner than she had ever undertaken before and wanted to be free to oversee the details. She was happy with his eagerness, but said, "You must content yourself with a few words after church, sir. Dinners don't put themselves on the table, you know."

He was a little hurt that she should put the preparation of a party before enjoying his company. "Isn't that what servants are for?" he replied.

"Yes, and if I had as many servants as you, I could leave the whole to them. Unfortunately I don't. I shall do the centerpiece myself." She didn't add that she would have to do a deal more besides, such as check the laying of the table and arrange a grande toilette for herself.

"I am quite a dab at arranging flowers," he tempted.

"Some gentlemen don't know how to take no for an answer," she said, to finish the subject.

"And I, Miss Beddoes, am one of that objectionable sort. Forewarned is forearmed."

On this charming piece of flirtation, they parted. Lettie went to the morning parlor, where Miss Millie had decided to have the bonnets and pelisses stored. Havergal loitered in the hallway beyond, waiting to see the guests off and hopefully to have a last word with Lettie. Crymont approached him before taking his leave.

"Old Norton seems to think I shall be visiting his swinery tomorrow, Havergal. I have told him twice I shan't, but the man seems to be deaf in one ear. Pray make my apologies if the subject comes up."

"I'll do that."

"I don't know how you can stand it, rusticating here at the height of the Season. Why don't you come back to London with me?"

"I shall be going to London soon. Business at the House. I am on a tariffs committee."

"Good God! Next you'll be telling me you are going to marry and settle down. The last infirmity of noble minds, milord."

"Not for a while," Havergal smiled, hoping to get Crymont out the door before Lettie came out.

"You won't forget, you're to join me at the inn later. I quite depend on you."

"I'll be there, never fear."

He looked up and saw Lettie staring at him. She had heard their last remarks and was pale with emotion. She walked stiffly forward. "Good evening, gentlemen. It was nice to see you again, Crymont." She gave a barely perceptible nod in Havergal's direction, and got hold of Violet to leave before she lost control completely.

If her eyes were moist, the darkness of the carriage concealed it. Violet was so enthusiastic in her praise of the ball that she noticed nothing amiss.

"I am very tired. I'm going directly to bed," Lettie said as soon as they were home.

"I told Siddons to lock up before I left, so that he would not have to stay up till two o'clock. I'll just check the doors to see he did it. Good night, Lettie."

In her room, Lettie lit one lamp and fell onto her bed, exhausted. So he was going to meet Crymont at the inn. He had no thought of marrying "for a while." He had not changed in the least, except to add deceit to his bag of tricks. At least he used to be frank about his wretched character. All this dissimulation! What was the point of it? He had been happy to see Crymont arrive, whatever he might say about having broken with his set. Very likely he had arranged it himself. Oh, Norton would be eager to abet him, of course, but Crymont had no opinion of Norton. It was Havergal he came to see. To meet at the inn, certainly with the lightskirts in tow again. The name Iona had surfaced more than once during supper, through the babble of other voices. Why else would Havergal go there at such an hour of the night, and after a particularly strenuous day, too?

Why had he feigned displeasure at Crymont's visit? Did he have some deep plan for getting his money out of her? Was that it? Paint himself as a reformed character, flirt a little, and she would hand it over, all of it? His father had apparently been taken in by the ruse. Five thousand he had got, and she could not believe it was safely invested. More likely he had bought a bunch of showy horseflesh, as Crymont mentioned.

Treachery and deceit at every turn. He had never cared for her at all. And tomorrow she was having an elaborate dinner party in honor of this deceiver. At least it would be a going-away party. He left on Monday, and that saddened her, too. It was some hours later that she remembered she had told Tom to be sure to call on Havergal in London. She must write and counter that order. Tom would think she had run mad, changing her mind so often. Speak to Crymont but not Havergal. Speak to Havergal but not Crymont. And now, don't have anything to do with either of them. She would follow the advise she gave to Tom. Have nothing to do with either of them. Forget them and just go on with her life.

What a wretched life it would be, with Violet gone, and Tom settled permanently in London. That thought called up memories, too, of Havergal's strange insistence that she go to London. Not home to meet his family, but to London for a tawdry flirtation. Of course! The firm handling the trust was in London! How convenient to arrange the handing over of the monies. Her heart hardened to consider his treachery.

And to think, she had to endure dinner with him tomorrow without telling him exactly what she thought of him. She would never be able to do it. She would just have to send a note to Norton Knoll canceling the dinner. She couldn't face the ordeal.

Chapter Sixteen

Lᴇᴛᴛɪᴇ ᴅɪᴅ ɴᴏᴛ have to pretend to be ill the next morning. Her cheeks were fevered, and when she lifted her head from the pillow, the dull ache between her temples throbbed like a drum.

"We shall cancel our dinner party," Violet decided when she rushed into Lettie's room to see what kept her abed on such an important day and saw her friend's pale face. "You are ill, dear. How very vexing for you."

"I'll be fine," Lettie said, and tried to smile.

"Back into bed with you, miss. I am in charge now, and I say we cancel the party," Violet repeated, straightening the coverlet around Lettie's shoulders.

"I am sorry, Violet. Really I don't feel well enough—"

"I should say you don't. You're as white as paper. I'm calling for the doctor this instant."

A ragged voice called out, "No!" Then it continued more restrainedly, "That is not necessary, thank you. It is just my nerves and all these unaccustomed late nights. I hate to think of all that food going to waste and all Cook's work. Don't cancel

174

the party, unless you fear you cannot handle it alone."

"Of course I can do it alone, for the arrangements are already made." Violet peered hopefully to the pale face on the pillow. "I cannot like to abandon you to the servants, however."

"I'm not fit for company today, Violet. I shan't require anything but an occasional cup of tea and some fingers of toast. Really, I would rather be alone, for my head throbs so." Hostessing the party would keep Violet out of her hair. All Lettie wanted was to be alone.

"I'll proceed with the party then, after I bring you some headache powders. With luck you may feel well enough to join us by dinnertime, or at least by evening. You will want to say good-bye to Havergal. He is leaving tomorrow, you know."

"Yes, I know," Lettie said in a dying voice.

Violet did not attend the service at St. Mary's Church that morning. Her absence caused Mr. Norton some worry. Havergal was less concerned about Lettie's absence. Parties do not throw themselves, she had told him, and no doubt she was busy. He thought it intrusive of Norton to call at Laurel Hall after church, but there was no preventing him. Miss Millie was along, and rather than sit alone in the carriage, Havergal went in with them.

Violet had soon explained matters to them. "Lettie has a touch of migraine and is in bed. She says she will not attend the party this evening, but I hope I can persuade her to."

"This laddie here is the one who could do it for you, Vi," Norton said, smiling at Havergal. "He has only to bat an eyelash and all the girls come trotting. I have noticed Lettie doesn't glare at him as she used to." He turned to Havergal. "Why don't you just nip up and give her arm a twist, laddie?"

"I never met a lady yet who wanted to be seen

when she was feeling under the weather," he replied, "but I'll send up a note, if I may, Miss FitzSimmons?"

"The very thing," Violet smiled, and led him to the study to compose his note.

Havergal knew she had been annoyed with him last night, but felt sure it was merely a fit of pique. Explaining it all in a note would take too long. He would do his explaining in person tomorrow when she was feeling stouter. He just dashed off a few lines.

The note was delivered, and Lettie took it with trembling fingers. "Dearest Lettie," she read. "I am sorry to hear you are not well. Too much trotting for one of your retired habits is, no doubt, the culprit. By all means stay in bed if you aren't up to another party, but may I call on you tomorrow before I leave? Best regards, and sincere love, Jacob."

Her lips trembled, then firmed in an angry line. She got up from bed and went to her writing desk. Across the bottom of his note she wrote, "You misjudge the culprit. It is not an excess of trotting but an excess of Lord Havergal's duplicity. Please do not call tomorrow, for I do not wish to see you. L. A. Beddoes."

She rang her bell and had the note taken below before she changed her mind. As soon as it was gone, she wished she had answered on a separate sheet, for she wanted to read his words again. "Dearest Lettie," he had written, not just "Dear Lettie." And the closing, too, with the mention of love. . . . What a fool she was to think that meant anything. She returned to bed, but between excitement and anger, she knew sleep was impossible.

Below, Havergal awaited her reply in the study. Hoping for some meaningful message, he preferred to read it in private. He read her curt, insulting words, scrawled on the bottom of his own returned note, and turned pale. Was it a joke? He soon realized it was not. This was her reaction to Crymont's turning up last night. As if that were *his* fault! It was Norton who invited him. Pride soon tinged his shock with anger, and when he joined the others, he said stiffly, "Had we not best be going, Ned? Miss Violet will have her hands full today."

"Miss Lettie failed to succumb to your note, eh? That surprises me, but we shall see her at the head of her table this evening if I know anything."

Several minutes later Havergal finally succeeded in getting Norton and Miss Millie out the door. His decision to leave for Willow Hall that same day was taken en route home. What was the point of hanging on? Lettie had let him know in no uncertain terms how she felt about him. An excess of Lord Havergal's duplicity, indeed! She treated him as if he were a libertine. Leaving would require an unexceptional excuse, for he did not wish to offend his host. A pity there was no post on Sunday. But that letter he had from Papa on Friday—he might pretend he hadn't perused it thoroughly. . . .

Norton tried in vain to detain Havergal, but didn't really mind that he was leaving. To arrive at Laurel Hall without him would cause a greater stir, and he alone would be the one who knew all the ins and outs of it. Havergal was worried at staying away from home so long. Tomorrow was his Uncle Harold's birthday—Havergal had overlooked it, in the rush of pleasures his host provided, but he had been rereading his Papa's last letter and come across the reminder. He would make a good story out of it, mentioning Havergal's concern at traveling on the Sabbath. To cap it all, there was his invitation to Willow Hall in a month's time. That was as good as an invitation to meet the Prince Regent in Norton's humble view.

The party was a merry one, despite Lord Havergal's defection and Miss Beddoes's absence. Echoes of conversation and laughter floated up to Lettie's chamber from below, telling her she was little missed. It was not till the party was over and Violet came to her to report on it that she learned Havergal had not attended.

"What excuse did he give?" Lettie demanded.

"He had to go home—an uncle's birthday, I believe."

"He deserted our party for that paltry excuse—traveling on a Sunday as well?"

"He was worried about that. Ned mentioned it two or three times."

"I don't believe a word of this faradiddle. He had made a rendezvous to meet Crymont. That is why he left."

"I cannot think so, Lettie, for they all—Havergal, Ned, and Millie—saw Crymont heading for London on their way to church. That was *hours* before Havergal left. He has invited Ned to Willow Hall in a month's time. Ned is very excited about it. Such an honor!"

"I don't see much honor in being used as a free expert in setting up the hog operation."

Violet gave her friend a rebukeful glance, but blamed this display of ill manners on the headache. "Ned is happy in any case, and I am happy for him."

Over the following days, word of Havergal's doings eventually seeped back to Laurel Hall. Norton corresponded with the viscount and brought each letter for the ladies to peruse. Havergal had a fair idea they would fall into Lettie's hands and composed his epistles with her in mind. They were a litany of worthy doings, including a purely apocryphal account of his Uncle Harold's seventieth birthday, after which he immediately dashed to

London to resume committee work at Whitehall. When being worthy had no effect, which is to say no apology from Lettie, he decided to try jealousy and invented a Lady Annabelle, whom he fictitiously escorted to various social dos. She was the daughter of a Scottish lord, a petite blonde, to make her as different from Lettie's statuesque brunette type as possible.

All of this was highly vexing to Lettie. She remembered Lord Cauleigh saying his son was thinking of marriage. Was it even remotely possible Havergal had been thinking of offering for herself? Surely his behavior suggested it. But the likelier explanation was that he was only trying to con his twenty-five thousand out of her. As she had refused, he was marrying an heiress instead.

Soon a matter of greater concern arose. Tom had always been expensive and, naturally, settling into a career in London required extra money. Funds had been set aside for this and were turned over to him. Although Tom had reached his maturity the winter before and was in charge of his own estate, from long habit their family man of business, Mr. Telford, kept Lettie in touch with matters. He called at Laurel Hall toward the end of May, wearing a worried frown. He was not a worrier by nature. Since her father's death, he had been calling frequently in the way of business, and when Lettie thought of him, she saw in her mind's eye a broad, smiling face, dancing brown eyes, and a rotund figure.

"I thought we ought to have a word," he said when he was shown in on that sunny afternoon.

"I hope nothing is amiss, Mr. Telford!" she exclaimed, noticing his mood.

"Not amiss, exactly. The estate is Tom's. Naturally he may do as he wishes with it, but I am a little concerned at his spending. I have already given him a hefty advance, and now he wants me to sell off the orchards. Twenty acres of prime fruit trees. It seems a shame. Has he discussed it with you?"

"Sell the orchard? *No!*" Lettie exclaimed, staring in disbelief.

"Oh my!" Miss FitzSimmons said, clutching at her heart. "The trees are so pretty in spring." Ever the optimist, she added, "But we shall still see the blossoms. It is not as though the buyer will chop them down."

"No, he mustn't sell," Lettie said firmly. "Papa would not have approved."

"It is his not getting a position," Violet said. "I expect it is very dear, living in London."

"Not that expensive," Lettie objected. "He has a good income from the estate, and he has hired modest rooms. He decided against setting up a carriage, though even that should have been possible from the monies we had set aside. What excuse did he give, Mr. Telford?"

"He mentioned some debts he must discharge immediately. Tradesmen would agree to monthly payments. I fear—now I don't wish to alarm you, ladies, but the thought does just arise that it might be gambling debts."

"Good God!" Lettie said, staring in horror.

"The exigent nature of the demand leads me to fear it," Telford explained. "A gentleman cannot delay paying his gambling debts. Young and inexperienced lads are pushed into foolish behavior to save their reputations."

"I know it well," Lettie said. An image of Havergal rose up in her mind. "I wish Papa had left the estate under my control till Tom was older."

"He was always a steady boy—sensible," Violet reminded her. "Oh, extravagant in little ways, like wanting sugarplums and new waistcoats, but nothing like gambling. He must have fallen into poor company in London."

Lettie knew only too well what vile company abounded there. Knaves like Havergal and Crymont.

"I do think your father ought to have delayed handing over the whole to Tom," Mr. Telford said, "but as Tom is the legal owner now, I must do as he says, Miss Beddoes. I shall be stopping at the estate agent's office when I return to town to list the orchard for sale. I just wanted to warn you, in case you didn't know. I hope you can talk some sense into the lad."

"Thank you for coming. I appreciate it." He left, still wearing his frown.

"You must write him a stiff letter, Lettie," Miss FitzSimmons declared. Almost on the same breath she decided to consult Ned in this matter. If nothing else, he would be happy to buy the orchard at a high price and save them the shame of having a FOR SALE sign posted on the property.

"Of course," Lettie agreed, still stunned from the news.

Violet called the carriage and darted off at once to consult with Ned. Lettie declined to join her. She would stay home to write the letter. It was difficult to summon the words hard enough to tell Tom what she thought of his behavior. Half a dozen discarded sheets littered the waste basket before she realized she must go in person to lecture him. She had to be there and see just how badly dipped Tom was. It was too easy to prevaricate in a letter. She put her pen aside and went to her room to begin packing. She would leave that very day.

When Violet returned, she had Ned and Miss Millie with her. "So Tom has gone to the bad," Norton said, shaking his head mournfully. "I always thought you were too soft by half with the lad, but

181

it was none of my concern if you spoiled him rotten. Never fear, Lettie, we will straighten him out."

Lettie's objection died on her lips. He was right. She had been too soft on Tom. She ought to have insisted he live within his means, instead of supplying the extra from her own allowance. And recently she had hardly given Tom a moment's thought from head to toe of the week. Her mind was too full of her own concern over Havergal.

"Indeed we shall. I am leaving for London at once to see him," she replied.

"I figured we'd head out tomorrow morning," Norton parried. "Get an early start, and with my bloods we'll be there before dark. I know Vi and you would dislike putting up at a country inn. Now in London, I always stay at Reddishes Hotel. I can recommend it. Comfortable and respectable, but not dear. You will feel right at home."

"I wouldn't dream of putting you to so much bother, Ned," Lettie said.

"Ho, bother! There is nothing I like better than an excuse to dash up to London. I go every chance I get. I will feel hurt if you don't let me tag along. You will be more comfortable having a man with you," he added kindly.

A trip to London was an enormous undertaking for Lettie, who had only been there twice before in her life. She remembered it as an overwhelming metropolis. Her own ancient carriage and team would not make it in one day, and once there, she had very little notion what hotel to put up at. All her servants were equally unsophisticated.

He saw her indecision and rushed in to settle the matter. "Now, what time shall we leave? Is seven-thirty too early for you? I am always up with the birds. It is no odds to me."

"If you're sure you don't mind, Ned . . ."

"Seven-thirty it is. I'll leave now and let you pack

up your gowns. Bring along a pretty one, for there is no saying we won't want to go out and celebrate after we have settled young Tom's hash."

Miss Millie hadn't spoken a word. Lettie asked if she would be joining them on the trip, and she said, "Only if you need me, Miss Lettie. I find travel fagging."

"I'm sure Ned will handle everything." Lettie smiled. "You are both so very kind."

Violet added her thanks, and the guests left. "I do like a man who takes charge," Violet said rather smugly.

"I hope you didn't ask for his help, Violet. Such an imposition."

"He offered before I could ask it."

"Yes, he would. I feel much better knowing he will be along to help us."

After the Nortons left, she drove into Ashford to the bank and took out most of the money in her account. One hundred and fifty pounds. She feared it would not begin to pay Tom's debts. She also knew what sacrifice she must make. When she got home, she took out her diamond necklace and examined it. It was her one piece of significant jewelry. Her father had given it to her mother as a wedding gift. It was not a grand or gaudy thing; it was estimated to be worth five hundred pounds. She hoped that would pay Tom's debts without selling the orchard. But the money would be only a loan. She would insist that Tom repay her every penny. No more spoiling him.

The afternoon and evening passed slowly. She was thankful to have the planning and packing to distract her, and thankful, too, for Mr. Norton's kind, unquestioning help. One liability to Norton's escort did occur to her, however. He was in correspondence with Havergal. She must caution him he was not to draw Havergal into the affair.

Lettie mentioned this as soon as they were comfortably ensconced in the carriage the next morning.

"I didn't write to him about it," Norton said. "It occurred to me that I might have him look Tom up and speak to him, but then I just had a doubt. . . . "

"What do you mean, Ned?" Violet demanded.

"Havergal mentioned calling on Tom. I had a niggling worry that he might be the cause of Tom's problem. Oh, he would never do any harm intentionally. He is the best-natured creature in the universe, but dropping a thousand at the gaming table would be nothing to Havergal. If Tom is racketing around with his set . . . I kept that letter from you to save worry."

"I warned Tom to have nothing to do with him!" Lettie said, chagrined.

"Havergal only mentioned it once. He is the one who called on Tom, so there is no need to be in the boughs with your brother. Tom did not seek out the acquaintance. It is just a thought. No doubt I am stirring up a hornet's nest for no reason. Pray forget I spoke, Lettie."

Far from forgetting it, it preyed on Lettie's mind constantly. By the time they reached London, she was half convinced Havergal had set out to ruin Tom on purpose, to spite her.

The evenings lingered long in May, but the shadows were lengthening as they entered the city, and when they pulled up in front of Reddishes, it was dark. Both Lettie and Violet were burned to the socket. They agreed that they would just have something to eat and retire, and begin their salvation of Tom in the morning. "For I am too fagged to be as harsh on him tonight as I wish," Lettie said.

She did look spent. Her face was pale and drawn from worry and an endless day of travel.

"An excellent idea, ladies," Norton agreed. "You both look like dishrags. I am never overcome by travel. I find it exhilarating. I will just step out on the town and meet you for breakfast. Say, nine o'clock. I will bespeak a private parlor. Ask for Norton's parlor when you come down. I shall pick up a journal and see what treats London offers."

With many bows and much kindness, he took his leave.

"If that man has not proposed yet, Violet," Lettie said, "I strongly suggest you ask him to marry you, immediately."

Violet colored up prettily and said, "He has, actually. We have been cudgeling our brains to think how to arrange it. Miss Millie insists she will leave Norton Knoll. I do not want her to in the least. We thought she might take over the swinery. She still thinks of it as home, you know, and she likes that idea."

Lettie was a little surprised that the romance had reached the boil so quickly. "What is causing the delay then?"

"Well, it is *you*, Lettie," Violet said, smiling apologetically. "I cannot leave you alone. Do you think perhaps Cousin Germaine, from Exeter, might like to live with you?"

"Yes, the very thing," Lettie said. "As soon as we get home, we shall begin work on the wedding." Cousin Germaine was the last lady in the land Lettie would want to share a house with. She was a tart-tongued spinster set in her ways, but there were other relatives who Lettie found more congenial, and she didn't want to discuss it at this time.

"Yes, I thought Germaine was the very one, for you and she are really quite a bit alike," Violet smiled.

Lettie took that unintentional slight to bed with

her. Was that how Violet and Norton saw her? As an opinionated, bossy shrew? As she lay in bed, worrying, the weak thought intruded, was that how Havergal saw her?

Chapter Seventeen

THE PLAN SETTLED on, over breakfast the next morning in Mr. Norton's private parlor, was that Ned would drive to Tom's apartment and bring him to the hotel. Ned had been up since seven-thirty and had already taken his gammon and eggs.

"It will save you ladies running out to the carriage with your meal in your throats. You just relax and enjoy your fork work, and I'll have the lad here before your plates are empty."

"So very kind," Lettie said. She seemed to have turned into a parrot, forever repeating her gratitude to Norton. At times, she regretted having turned him off. What an extremely comfortable husband he would have made after all. But as she considered the full duties of a wife, she concluded that he would make an even better connection than husband.

Breakfast was a leisurely meal, and would have been enjoyable, were it not for the cloud Tom's improvidence threw over the table. The ladies had very little idea of the geography of London, but Norton had assured them he would be back within the hour. When that time had come and gone, and they could not force another drop of coffee into their mouths, Lettie suggested they wait in their rooms.

As they entered the hotel lobby, Norton came pelting in alone. "Was Tom not at home?" Lettie demanded. It seemed unlikely that a young man who had no position should be out of the house so early.

"His man said he had gone to visit a friend in the country for a few days, but he is expected back this morning. I left a note for him to come immediately to the hotel. It looks like we are stuck to cool our heels here till he comes. I shouldn't think he would come much before noon. We could hire a cab and have a squint at the city for a couple of hours, if you like. Dandy buildings as far as the eye can see and plenty of shops."

As much as Lettie appreciated Norton's help, she also wished for some privacy with her brother and took the decision to wait for Tom alone. It took a deal of persuasion, but finally she talked Violet into her bonnet and pelisse for a tour of the city with Norton, while she awaited Tom.

"We'll be back for lunch. I have kept the private parlor," Ned told her. "Just make yourself at home there. I have brought a couple of journals for you to scan, to kill the time. Order a bottle of wine or coffee—whatever you wish, Lettie."

The room was cozy, and Lettie decided to await Tom's arrival there. Her interest in politics was slight, and for amusement she turned to the social columns of the journals, thinking to learn what new parties Lord Havergal had been attending with Lady Annabelle. Strangely Havergal's face had disappeared from all the cartoons. The Duke of C—— appeared frequently by name. It seemed he had bought his mistress a set of cream ponies and a sky blue phaeton. He had forsaken pig racing for boxing. She read the list of coming matches and saw that Lord H's man, Cuttle, had a match scheduled for the next week. This suggested that the friendship between Havergal and Crymont continued.

After an hour she decided she could handle one more cup of coffee and called for it. At eleven she asked for biscuits, not because she wanted them, but because she was utterly bored. She ought to have brought some sewing or a long novel. At eleven-thirty she stood with her nose to the windowpane, searching the busy street beyond for a sign of Tom. When he finally appeared, she thought she must be imagining things. She was beginning to doubt that he would ever come.

She ran to the parlor door and called. "Over here, Tom!"

He came bolting forward, smiling and looking perfectly elegant in a jacket and waistcoat she had never seen before. He looked thinner and a trifle hagged. In fact, he looked suddenly no longer like a boy, but like a young man. His dark hair sat in a neat cap, and his brown eyes were sunk a little deeper in his face than she remembered. The face was thinner, too.

"What the deuce are you doing here, Lettie? I thought one of my friends was playing a joke on me when I got Mr. Norton's note. And how does it come he is with you?"

"He isn't with me, exactly. He is going to marry Violet."

"Really! When did this happen?"

"Just recently. Come in, Tom. We have to talk."

She led him into the parlor and poured him a cup of tepid coffee. "Tom, what is all this about selling the orchard?"

"Did old Telford tell you? I don't know why he can't mind his own business. Why must he run around, making a great to-do about nothing?"

"Selling off your patrimony is not *nothing*, Tom.

Now tell me why you need the money. You had a thousand pounds to see you through. You cannot have gone through all that!"

"Everything is dear in London," he said sulkily.

"Not that dear! Have you been gambling?"

"Where the devil did you get that idea? I suppose Telford told you that, too, did he?" He lowered his eyes over his cup, for he suddenly felt like a guilty boy who had been caught playing truant.

"Never mind who told me. How deeply are you dipped?"

"Selling the orchard would more than cover it. It would leave me a couple of hundred to go on with."

"So you are in hawk for something in the neighborhood of five hundred?" she asked.

"Yes."

"Five hundred squandered, on top of the thousand you had to begin with! At this rate, you will have lost Laurel Hall within a year. The estate that your father worked all his life to make prosperous for you! You should be well and thoroughly ashamed of yourself. You've been a month in London already and no sign of a position. I cannot think you've been bending your mind to finding one."

"Dash it, nobody works in London. You don't understand how things go on, Lettie. Everybody lives off his estate. I'm not a poor man. Why should I sit in an office, scribbling letters for some scheming politician?"

"You're not a rich man either. That life you talk about is for wealthy lords. I hear you have seen Lord Havergal?"

"And that's another thing," Tom said, turning to offense, as his defense was nonexistent. "You told me to call on him and the duke, then no sooner do I meet him than you tell me to stay clear of him. It is demmed hard, when he has been so kind to me, introducing me to his friends and getting me into his club."

"So that's it. You have been rattling around town with that expensive fribble. I'm telling you, Tom, you either find a position, or you are coming home."

"*I'm* the master of Laurel Hall now, my girl," he said, but his voice quavered with fear as he said it.

"We'll see about that. There is a good case to be made that you are too immature to handle your estate yet. I happen to know something about the laws of guardianship," she reminded him. "If a person is incapable of handling his own affairs, then it is possible for his next of kin to have herself declared guardian. You know Papa's intentions in turning it all over to you was that you *run* the estate, not *decimate* it. I'll do it, Tom. I won't sit still and see you ruin your life for a few months' debauchery. You'll thank me for it in the long run."

"Hardly debauchery," he said, sulking.

"I'm not talking about lightskirts, though I don't doubt your new friend has introduced you into that as well."

"It was only a bit of gambling," Tom said. "To tell the truth, Lettie, I thought we were playing for shillings, but when they say one, they mean one pound! My God, I nearly fainted when I discovered the truth. I ought to have known, for something similar happened at university, where one means one shilling, whereas at home it means one penny. I haven't been back to that club," he said as a sop.

"What club is it—Brook's, St. James's?"

"It was a private club, Mrs. Reno's place."

"A gambling hell, designed to fleece Johnnie Raws! You really *are* incompetent to handle your own affairs."

"It's all the crack, Lettie. All the fellows are dying to get in, but you have to be introduced by someone that Mrs. Reno knows and trusts. She serves champagne and lobster. The food and drinks alone are practically worth the price."

"Worth five hundred pounds? Worth losing a valuable piece of your estate? What will have to go next to pay for your vices—the stable, the pasture, the house? What are your plans for *after* you have ruined yourself? Do you plan to batten yourself on my meager ten thousand? Think again. I've spoiled you long enough. You got the lion's share of the family money, but you'll not see one sou of my dowry. And if you are thinking of a profitable marriage to pull you out of the suds, you can forget that dream. The wealthy merchants' daughters, I have no doubt your friend has mentioned to you, expect a title. They aren't interested in penniless country squires of poor character and reputation. No, Tom, you were wrong, and in your heart you know you were wrong."

"Damn, I know I was a fool, but that doesn't pay the bill, does it?" he exclaimed.

"Who do you owe the money to?" she asked, and braced herself for the answer.

"I borrowed it from a moneylender, a fellow named Wideman, on Poland Street. Here is his note."

She examined it and handed it back. "Very well, I'll tell you what we'll do. I shall sell my diamond necklace."

"No!"

"Laurel Hall obviously means more to *me* than it does to you. I would rather lose Mama's diamonds, and you know what they mean to me. This is not a gift. I will expect you to reimburse me for them, as though the money was a mortgage. In fact, we shall draw up a note, at five percent interest."

Tom's face screwed up and a few tears squirted out of his eyes. "I'm sorry, Lettie. I've been a demmed jackass. I feel so terrible. I was afraid to tell you. I *wanted* to. I knew you would think of something." He went into her arms, and in spite of her determination, she felt a weakening rush of love.

"It's all right, Tom. You're young. Too young for the pack of hardened rakes you've been running with."

"I'll go home with you, Lettie. Truth to tell, London ain't as much fun as I had hoped. Between worrying about money, and meeting all the pretty debs hanging out for a title and a big fortune, I haven't been having that good a time. At home, all the girls made a great fuss over me, but here I'm nothing. The apartment is a miserable dump, and the food is awful. I think I've lost a few pounds." She gave him a quizzing look. "Of body weight, I mean, besides the fortune I've squandered. Just like a Johnnie Raw. I ought to be whipped."

"Don't tempt me. Norton and Violet will be returning at noon. Let us—"

As she spoke, there was a commotion at the door, and Norton's booming voice rang out. "So he has come. I hope Lettie has rung a good peel over you."

"Indeed she has," Tom said with a shy smile. "And well deserved, too."

Violet rushed forward to greet Tom, and Norton turned to speak to Lettie aside. "I can let you have a few hundred if it will ease the strain, Lettie. Tom can pay me back at his leisure."

"The sum is not so great as I feared. I can handle it. Thank you once again, Ned."

"That's good then. Tonight I shall take you all to the theater and for a smashing dinner at a hotel to celebrate. Tom can tell us where to go."

"The Clarendon—No, this hotel is as good as any," Tom said with a thought to the prices.

"Tonight dinner is on me," Lettie announced, for

she felt guilty at Norton's unending generosity. Ned put up a good fight, but in the end Lettie had her way.

Over lunch, it was decided that Tom and Lettie would attend to business that afternoon, and Ned and Violet would continue their sight-seeing. Lettie wanted privacy for the selling of her necklace. Norton would insist on lending her the money if he knew what she planned, and she would not infringe further on his good nature.

Tom announced his intention of returning to Laurel Hall with them. "There, then that solves your problem, Lettie," Violet smiled. "You won't be alone when I marry Ned."

"I have not congratulated you, Mr. Norton, on your betrothal," Tom said, and rectified the omission.

"Since our little secret is out, I can put a diamond on my lass's finger this very day," Norton beamed. "That will be a pleasant job, finding a ring to fit."

Tom and Lettie remained behind when the others left. Tom said, "Lettie, I have been thinking . . . I don't want you to sell your necklace. Perhaps I can arrange a small mortgage on Laurel Hall."

"Small mortgages have a way of growing, Tom. It is so easy to increase them once the thing is started. Papa always said he would rather sell the coat off his back than take a mortgage. In a bad year, you know, a mortgage can make the difference in the estate's breaking even."

"Let me look into it at least. It won't take more than an hour. I'll just speak to an estate agent and see what sort of a deal I can arrange."

"Don't even think of it," she insisted.

"Well, at least I must go to my apartment and tell my man to pack. I know a fellow who is desperate for rooms. I'll call on him and sublet my place.

That'll give me a couple of hundred to settle a few accounts outstanding in town. My tailor, and the fellow I bought this new curled beaver from," he said, smiling ruefully at his new hat.

Lettie was happy to hear that he wanted to settle his accounts before leaving town. That augered a good character beneath the recent folly. Tom had always been a basically good lad.

"Don't do anything about selling the necklace till I return," he said as he went toward the door.

Lettie pondered this speech. She knew Tom well enough to know that he planned to try for a mortgage. It was sweet of him to want to save her necklace, but she had taken the decision to sell it and had every intention of doing so.

"I'll be gone for two or three hours," he said. "Don't wait for me. Hire a cab and go out and see the sights, Lettie."

Unlike taking a mortgage, selling diamonds was relatively easy. She could get the money within the hour and pay off his troublesome note. She would have felt better with an escort, but she was mature enough to tackle the city without one.

She called for a cab and asked to be delivered to Bond Street, where she made inquiries about the sale of her necklace at three establishments, finally returning to the first one, which had offered five hundred. She felt a piercing sadness to lay her beloved heirloom on the counter. What lady would be wearing it next? She hoped it did not end up on the neck of some lightskirt. After some discussion the shop agreed to pay her in cash. Her next destination was Mr. Wideman, on Poland Street. In the cab she remembered that she ought to have gotten Tom's IOU, but she would get a receipt from Wideman, and that would be proof the note was discharged—probably with a forfeit of several pounds.

The driver looked curious when she gave the address, but the lady certainly looked as if she knew what she was about. Lettie felt a few qualms as the carriage proceeded into a fairly squalid part of town. There were no trees and few carriages, but only run-down houses packed close together, with a few down-at-heels gentlemen walking the street.

"Wait for me," she said curtly when she got out. She surveyed the mean establishment. It was an apartment buiding, one of a row a block long, with only a small brass plaque to inform clients of the various matters going on within. As well as Wideman, there was also a solicitor, no doubt a shady one, a dealer in coins, and an art merchant, whom she felt in her bones sold either stolen goods or forgeries.

She opened the door and stood, studying the list of businesses pasted in the hallway. Mr. Wideman was on the second floor. She gathered up her skirts, for the staircase looked as if it hadn't seen a broom in months. As she put her foot on the first step, she heard a rattle of descending footsteps. Their firm tread and rapid pace told her it was a young man. Some other unfortunate victim like poor Tom, perhaps. As the stairway was dark and narrow, she waited below till he had passed. God only knew what sort of man he might be. He might rob her of the fortune in her reticule.

She looked up as he negotiated the bend at the top of the stairs and felt as if her lungs had collapsed. Havergal! She thought she must be imagining things, for he had been so much in her thoughts. She blinked and looked again, just as he looked up and recognized her.

"Lettie!" The word came out in a shocked, disbelieving rasp.

All her grief and anger congealed into disgust. How could anyone who looked so good be so horrid? He looked as she remembered: young, handsome, healthy, prosperous. But he had caused her untold harm and had nearly ruined Tom into the bargain. And now he was here, probably selling off his birthright to pay for his latest sins.

"Lord Havergal," she replied in icy accents. "So it was you who directed Tom here. No doubt Mr. Wideman is an intimate business acquaintance of yours. Do you get a commission on the Johnnie Raws you send to him to be fleeced?" He just stared dumbly. "I will be taking Tom home tomorrow, before you turn him into another libertine like yourself."

"I didn't!"

"Do you deny that you called on him in London?"

"Of course not! I promised you I would help him find a position."

"You are either extremely ineffectual or have an odd idea of a position. Tom has to earn money, not throw it away on gambling. Excuse me." She made a movement to walk past him.

He still looked stunned, but he recovered enough to become angry. His eyes flashed dangerously, and his lips were white. He didn't trust himself to speak. He just pushed a piece of paper into her hand before he strode to the door, without having said one word in his own defense.

Lettie felt faint when he left. She leaned against the wall, panting. It was a moment before she noticed the paper in her fingers. She unfolded it and saw it was Tom's note for five hundred pounds, discharged. Wideman had scrawled "Paid in Full" with his signature. How had this happened? What was Havergal doing with the note? She went to the carriage and asked to be taken to Reddishes Hotel.

She pondered the matter as the carriage moved sluggishly through the streets. Tom must have arranged the mortgage against her wishes, and for some reason Havergal was discharging the debt for him. Perhaps to save time, as Tom had a deal of business to attend to and was now eager to get home. Tom and Havergal were obviously seeing each other regularly. Havergal must be feeling guilty now that she was here in town, catching him in the very act of seducing Tom. If he thought performing this small errand was enough to redeem his black character, he had another thought coming. She would make Tom pay off the mortgage with her five hundred pounds before they left town.

And she would warn him he was never to speak the words Lord Havergal within her hearing again.

Chapter Eighteen

LETTIE DARTED INTO the hotel, holding back her tears till she reached the privacy of her room. Tom came out of Norton's private parlor to greet her.

"The greatest luck, Lettie. Beau Mason was delighted to get my apartment. He paid me cash on the line for the whole season's rent. They make you pay by the quarter when you sign up."

She followed him into the parlor, relieved to see they were alone. Curiosity was blended in plentiful supply with her grief, and she demanded, "Tom, what was Lord Havergal doing with your IOU?"

"Eh? How the deuce did you know he had been here?"

She stared, curiosity mounting higher. "He was *here*?"

"He landed in the moment I arrived. I've been waiting for you this past three quarters of an hour. I paid off my tailor and the hatmaker, and came straight around to tell you. My man is packing up my belongings."

"But where did you meet Havergal?"

"I already told you, he was here, looking for you. He ran into Norton and Violet on Bond Street, and they told him you were here."

Strange sensations whirled in her brain. He was looking for *her*! He had come to see her. For one fleeting instant her heart soared, then the outcome of their eventual meeting flooded over her. "That doesn't explain how he got your note?" she said in confused accents.

"He doesn't have it. It's right here." He began digging into his pockets, then searching around the table and floor. "It *was* here. I showed it to him. That old bleater of a Norton told him why you were all here. 'Young Tom is in a spot of trouble,' he said. Never can hold his tongue. Havergal asked me about it, and—"

"I should hardly think it necessary for Havergal to inquire, when he is the one who led you to Mrs. Reno to be fleeced."

"Havergal? Good Lord, it wasn't Havergal. It was the duke. I only saw Havergal the one time when he called on me, offering to help me find a position. I had had your letter warning me off from him, so I treated him pretty stiff and didn't repay his call."

Lettie experienced a dryness in her throat, and a dull ache in her heart. "I also warned you away from the duke," she said.

"I didn't go looking for him, but when we chanced to meet one day on the strut, he was so pleasant and friendly, telling me how he was a great friend of yours and Norton's and all, that there was no getting away from him. I couldn't remember just at the moment whether he wasn't the one I was supposed to look up. He insisted on treating me to dinner at his club. The duke told me Havergal isn't quite the thing nowadays. Used to be the prime sport in town, but he's changed. I could see for myself it was true. Havergal didn't talk of anything but finding a position. I can't see myself being locked up in a dusty office for days on end, especially in spring," he added, looking out the window.

Lettie sank onto a chair, too weak to argue. "How did Havergal get this?" she said, and handed him the discharged IOU.

Tom examined it, frowning. "Damn, Lettie, I told you not to sell your necklace. It was very kind of you to pay my IOU, but I wish you hadn't done it. I had decided to arrange the mortgage after we get home. My property is known around Ashford, and it would be easier to get the blunt from our own banker. Now we'll have to come back to London to get your diamonds, unless we can arrange it by mail."

"I didn't discharge the note. Havergal did. He was there, at Wideman's. He gave it to me."

Tom rubbed his ear and furrowed his youthful brow. "I don't see how the devil he got it. I showed it to him when I was explaining my 'spot of trouble,' as Norton so kindly blabbed to him. Old maid."

"He is a very good friend, Tom. Don't speak so harshly of Ned, if you please."

"It's the first time I ever heard you say a good word about him," he reminded her. "Havergal must have pocketed the note when I wasn't looking. But why did he discharge it? I turned down his offer of a loan. He gave a curious look when I told him I was afraid you meant to sell your diamonds. He left right after that, now that I think of it. I say, Lettie, there isn't a match brewing between the pair of you, is there? I don't see why else he would—"

"No, there is not."

"I didn't think so. I mean, he is rather young. . . ."

Another shaft entered her heart. "We must repay him at once."

"But why did he do it?"

"I have no idea. You must take this five hundred from my diamonds and repay him, Tom. I won't be indebted to him."

"I don't even know where he lives. *He* is the one who called on *me*."

"On Berkeley Square," Lettie said in a hollow voice. "If he is not there, leave the money and a note, thanking him."

"Well of course I'll thank him, though I think it demmed encroaching of him to have gone darting off without a word to me. He must have done it for *you*. I scarcely know the man. Shouldn't you write a note as well, Lettie? I mean he obviously meant well. And what about your diamonds?"

"Damn the diamonds. I hope I never see them again either," she said, and broke into tears.

Tom studied her a moment in silence, then went forward and led her to the sofa, where he patted her head and felt very mature. Poor old Lettie, she was never prone to vapors. Must be getting unsettled in her old age. "Never mind, old girl. I'll get it all straightened out."

Lettie looked up with watery eyes. "Tell him— Oh, never mind. What's the use? He'll never have me now."

Tom stared. It seemed entirely unlikely that a top-of-the-trees buck like Havergal would give Lettie a second look, but he had paid the note. Must be something afoot between them. Odd Havergal hadn't mentioned it. "I know your sister," he had said, or something cold like that. Not "I want to marry your sister." Tom would have remembered that.

"The money is in here," Lettie said, and handed Tom her reticule.

He found the money and the chit for Lettie's sale of the necklace. He wanted to redeem it before they left London and took the chit. Maybe Norton would lend him the blunt. Yes, going to marry Violet after all. Practically family, and he would insist on paying interest, get it all drawn up legally.

"Righto then, I'll be back in two shakes. Now buck up, Lettie. There is nothing as unsightly as a watering can. Why don't you go upstairs and have a lie down till Violet returns?"

"Yes, I'll do that," Lettie said, and dragged herself up from the chair. Tom handed her her reticule, and she went upstairs.

The room was not large or beautiful, but she knew from the night before that the bed was comfortable, and she lay on it, gazing up at the ceiling. Havergal had not led Tom astray, as she had thought. He had tried to help Tom. It was Crymont who had done the mischief. It was clear now that Havergal had really cut his friendship with the duke. Whatever had transpired at the inn the night of Norton's ball, when Havergal agreed to meet Crymont there, it might have been innocent. She should have asked Jacob.

Jacob. The name was a luxury she hadn't allowed herself since Havergal had left Ashford. Since she had dismissed him, to put it in plain Anglo-Saxon. She had accused him without anything but circumstantial evidence. How cold and vindictive he must think her. Accusing him rashly, when he had been trying to help Tom and her. Hot tears ran down from her eyes to moisten the pillow. And she hadn't even sent a note of apology with Tom. She must do so at once. Perhaps he would call before they left London. . . .

When she remembered his frozen face the last time she saw him, she didn't think he would call. A man could only take so much abuse. She had lost Norton, too, by her indifference. "It's the first time I ever heard you say a good word about him." She was glad that Tom was coming home, but it would be only a matter of time before Tom found himself a bride, and obviously he wouldn't want a shrew like herself in the house.

Laurel Hall didn't have a dower house. Perhaps Tom would build her a small one. . . . She wouldn't need much space—all alone.

An hour passed before Violet joined her, smiling and chattering like a magpie about the shops, dear Ned, and the sweet ring he had bought her. She held out her left hand, where a large diamond sparkled on her third finger. Lettie summoned her resources to make the proper show of delight and deliver her compliments.

"He is taking us all out to the theater after dinner tonight. Tom is coming with us. Isn't it exciting, Lettie? We like London so much we have decided to have our honeymoon here."

Lettie smiled and nodded, then prepared her announcement. She had a migraine and would not be joining the party that night. Violet's next speech reminded her that that cowardly course was not open to her. "So kind of you to treat us to this dinner, Lettie. But you know Ned won't let us pay a penny of the cost of this trip, so it is a way to repay him. I shouldn't be surprised if we find our hotel bill already paid when we leave."

"We mustn't let him do that!" Lettie exclaimed, and said nothing about her migraine.

"Try if you can stop him! What are you wearing tonight?"

"I brought my bronze taffeta."

"Excellent, and I shall wear my green, with the new fringed shawl I bought this afternoon."

They both began the arduous task of preparing for an unaccustomed evening at the theater. The only reference to Tom and his debt was a few brief sentences.

"Tom told me it is all settled, about his debt," Violet said.

"Yes, we got it straightened out. He is so eager to return to Laurel Hall."

"So he said! I think it is for the best. And you will have someone to stay with now. Things couldn't have worked out better."

"Yes."

"I understand Havergal was involved somehow." Lettie acknowledged it with a half smile, unable to speak. "Ned wanted to ask him to the theater with us, but it was impossible to get another seat on such short notice."

"That's too bad," Lettie said, and felt vastly relieved. She was also curious to hear what Tom had to say about his visit to Berkeley Square. "Tom is back then, is he?"

"He was, but he had to dart out to recover his evening clothes. He will be changing in Ned's room and meet us downstairs."

This arrangement made it difficult to have a private word with Tom, but she would get him aside at the first opportunity. This occurred while Ned was consulting the waiter about wine before dinner. "Was Havergal at home?" she asked in a low voice. Tom nodded. "What did he have to say?"

"He just accepted the money and my thanks. Seemed a tad chilly, I thought."

No wonder, Lettie added to herself. Dinner and the theater after seemed unreal and unending. Lettie was there in body, smiling and trying to add a few words to the conversation, but her mind was far away, repining over her lost chance for happiness. After the theater Norton insisted on taking them to a hotel for more supper.

"This is what I call a fine evening. What do you all say to staying over for another day?" he said as they finally prepared to leave the supper table.

"Oh no!" Lettie exclaimed weakly.

"The thing is, Lettie, Vi wants to pick up a few trifles for her trousseau," Ned explained. "I have a couple of things to do myself. I would like to get

205

measured for a proper London jacket for my wedding—it seems a waste to have to come back again when we are already here. Another day would do it. There is no great yank to get home, is there?"

"No, but—"

He said in a low voice, "If it is the cost that deters you, don't give it a thought. It will be my treat."

"That's not necessary—really."

"I would like to make a few calls and say goodbye to some of my friends," Tom said.

Suddenly it was decided. They were to remain another day. Lettie felt as if she had been given a life sentence.

She saw and heard, as if from a great distance, Violet's mouth saying, "You may want to do some shopping yourself, Lettie. You will stand as my bridesmaid, I hope?"

"Always a bridesmaid; never a bride," Norton joked. "Just funning, Lettie. You will be snapped up before the summer is out. Mark my words."

Lettie was obliged to smile and accept this leveler in good spirits.

Chapter Nineteen

THE LONG, DEEP breaths from the pillow beside her told Lettie that Violet was enjoying a peaceful sleep. Lettie lay in the darkness, staring at the rectangle of window, where a wan ray of moonlight penetrated through the closed draperies. The subject that occupied her mind was whether the day that just passed was the worst day of her life, or whether the Sunday she had stayed away from her own luncheon party exceeded it in grief.

She decided that the more recent day took the palm, for it lacked even the counter-irritant of anger to help assuage her grief. This entire muddle was all her own fault. She must swallow her pride and write an apology to Havergal before she left the city. As sleep was impossible, she spent some time mentally composing the epistle and rose early the next morning to put it to paper while Violet was still asleep.

But when she sat down to write, she was nervous at being caught out and forgot all her high-flown phrases. The message came from the heart. "Havergal," she wrote, after much soul-searching to decide between Jacob and Lord Havergal, or Dear Lord Havergal. "I am deeply sorry that I misjudged you. I was wrong, and I apologize." Once she began writing, the words came easily, as though she were speaking to him, holding nothing back. "I confess I had judged you before we ever met, taking my opinions from the journals and our occasional scuffle over your funds. Your first visit, if you remember, tended to reinforce my opinion. You changed, but my opinion did not, and at heart I was always ready to believe the worst of you. I appreciate your kindness on Tom's behalf and believe that you did it, at least in part, to please me. I would be very sorry to think I had totally lost that regard you once held, for your opinion matters a great deal to me. Sincerely, Lettie."

She read the note once, quickly, before sealing it up and sending it off via a servant to Norton's footman for delivery. Taking some action bolstered her confidence, and when the party met for breakfast, she agreed to spend the morning shopping with Violet while Ned ordered his new jacket and Tom sought out his friends. When they regrouped at the hotel for lunch, she made a discreet inquiry at the desk for an answer to her note. There was none. Havergal must surely have had it before he left home that morning. He had not forgiven her, then. She was sorry, but she could not blame him.

When plans were being laid for the afternoon, Lettie said she would like to be left off at Somerset House to view the spring exhibition of paintings. What she really wanted was not to be a nuisance to the lovers and to be alone to nurse her bruised spirits.

"We'll go with you," Norton said at once. "There is nothing I like better than to look at fine pictures. A half an hour to view, and—"

"You misunderstand, Ned. I would like to browse for hours. I am old enough to look after myself, and I shall take a hansom cab back to the hotel."

"That you will not. Just tell us how long you wish to gawk around, and we'll pick you up after."

"Two hours," she decided. That would get them home in time for tea. There would be only one more evening of this living hell, then she could get home and let her wound begin to heal.

"Perhaps Tom would like to go with you," Violet suggested.

"No, Tom is meeting his friends for one last outing before he goes home."

After many attempts at dissuasion, Lettie had her way and was let off at Somerset House. She was surprised at the enormous size of the place and the quantity of pictures hung higgledy-piggledy from ceiling to floor. They were nearly impossible to see for the crowds of art lovers. She let herself be carried along by the throng, seeing a corner of a painted wheat field here, the crossed legs of a gentleman farmer there, and occasionally gaining a glimpse of a whole painting high above her head. She didn't mind. The crowd and crush provided a diversion from her thoughts.

There was a grand staircase, presumably leading to more paintings abovestairs. Thinking that the upstairs gallery might be less crowded, she worked her way toward the stairs.

It was Lord Havergal's custom to arrive at the House at ten or shortly after in the morning. On that day, however, he planned to leave at noon, so he went to his office at eight. He missed Norton's footman by minutes. At work he was hardly aware of the complicated matters he studied. His mind kept straying to Lettie. After visiting five jewelry shops, he had found her diamonds and redeemed them with the five hundred pounds Tom had repaid him. He would send them to her hotel, and that was the last personal communication he would have with her. A rueful smile tugged at his lips. The second to the last. She would certainly repay him for the diamonds. And she would continue to forward his quarterly check from Uncle Horace's trust. Punctually on the dot. Miss Beddoes was as dependable as the tide.

What must she have made of him, with his lies and ruses, his drinking and his lightskirts? God, she must have thought Satan himself had invaded her orderly world. He admired her serenity and sense of order, but a lady could be too set in her ways, too narrow-minded, too judgmental. Damn, she could at least give him credit for trying. And damn the duke's eyes. Had she thought they were carrying on with lightskirts again? Surely she didn't have that poor an opinion of him!

He meant to send the diamonds to the hotel with a footman at noon. Whatever her plans for the morning, she would surely go to their hotel at noon to freshen up. The member of Parliament for his own riding chose twelve o'clock to call on Havergal and discuss riding matters. Allenbury was an excellent member, and he couldn't be treated shabbily. When Havergal finally got away and returned to Berkeley Square, it was one o'clock. He was handed Lettie's note at the door. "This arrived just after you left, Your Lordship."

He recognized her writing from countless business letters in the past, but it wasn't time for a check, and his heart began thumping in his throat. Now what had he done wrong? This would be some new shower of abuse, no doubt, or more likely a notice that she was discontinuing as guardian of Horace's trust.

He went to his study to read it in private and was undone by the simple sincerity of her words. Hope rose in his breast, and instead of sending the diamonds, he took them to Reddishes Hotel himself, envisaging a reconciliation. It was a disappointment to find the whole party was out. He decided to wait and went into the lobby. For a long ninety minutes he sat, not moving a limb, while his mind raced to the heights of hope, only to plunge in a moment to the depths of despair. In that ninety minutes he was turned off scornfully, married to Lettie, resumed his life of vice, and became a hermit, all without moving a limb.

When at last he spied Norton and Miss Fitz-Simmons entering, he dashed out to meet them. "Where is Lettie?" he demanded.

"We are just on our way to Somerset House to pick her up, as soon as Vi puts away her parcels. She wanted to see the pictures. Lettie is a great one for art," Norton added, though this was, in fact, the first manifestation of her love. "Will you join us, laddie, and we'll all stop somewhere for a glass of wine? It is dry work, shopping. We had a dandy time. Vi has bought out half the shops in London."

"You are tired," Havergal said at once. "Let me pick Lettie up and deliver her back here."

"That is mighty kind of you," Norton said, smiling. "We'll all go along."

Miss FitzSimmons saw the shadow pass over Havergal's face and said, "Oh do let us rest, Ned. I am fagged to death. We'll have a nice cup of tea in that parlor you keep standing ready for us, and Havergal and Lettie will join us later."

Norton would have preferred to be darting around town in a crested carriage, but he knew his fiancée's wishes must take precedence at this time and smiled obligingly. "Just as you wish, my dear. You'll join us for dinner, lad? We won't take no for an answer."

"I would like you all to join me at my house. I am deeply enough in your debt already, Ned."

"It would be a pleasure," Norton said. "I think

we can answer for Lettie and Tom as well, eh Vi? They would like it of all things. But we'll see you and Lettie here before that, I hope?"

"Certainly you will."

Havergal hurried off. "We might have gone with him," Ned mentioned, but just once and not in a condemning way.

"Oh Ned, you are blind as a bat. He is in love with her. Give them some privacy. You know love-birds want to be alone," she said, leading him to the private parlor.

"There is nothing nicer, though I shouldn't have minded taking a glimpse at those pictures."

Havergal was daunted by the crush of visitors at Somerset House. It seemed impossible to find Lettie amidst the swell of moving bodies. He didn't even know what she was wearing. He spent a few minutes looking over the tops of heads for a familiar bonnet, then his eyes were drawn to the grand staircase. He saw her, standing stock-still in the middle of her descent, staring at him as if she'd seen a ghost.

Lettie couldn't believe the evidence of her eyes. *He had come!* And in her heart she knew he had come for her, that he had discovered her where-abouts. She drifted down the stairs as he advanced toward her, both like souls in a trance. They met at the bottom of the staircase. Havergal reached for her hand and tucked it under his arm. "Ned told me you were here" is all he said, and even those few words sounded strained.

They left, still without speaking. There was so much to say, yet without a word being spoken, they both sensed that the crisis was at hand. It was not till they were in Havergal's carriage that Lettie said, "Did you receive my note?"

"Not till an hour ago. I left early for the House

this morning. I went to your hotel the minute I received it."

"I hope you aren't very angry with me?" she asked in a small voice.

She noticed then that he was squeezing her fingers painfully hard. "I was afraid you were going to drop the trust" was his reply.

This irrelevancy seemed perfectly clear to Lettie. "No, why should I?"

He gazed into her eyes. "Because I am—*unworthy* of your time and thought."

"Oh Jacob, don't say such things. I have behaved very badly to you, not trusting you. . . ."

"How could you trust a libertine such as I? Till I met you, I never gave a thought to anything but amusing myself. I have changed—"

She smiled a watery smile and found her finger touching his cheek. "I know, and I refused to see it. When you and Crymont were making that tryst at the inn . . ."

"Norton's ball," he nodded, covering the fingers on his cheek with his own and squeezing. "He just wanted me to vouch for his check with the proprietor. Ran himself into the ground at the Southampton races. Is that why you didn't come to your dinner party?" He took her hand and lifted it to his lips.

"I did have a migraine," she said, watching as his dark head bent over her fingers, his lips nibbling kisses.

Then he lifted his eyes, and she felt herself drowning in their bottomless depths. A slow smile grew on his lips. "I have that effect on a lot of people," he said. "Most particularly on *Mr*. Beddoes, I fear?"

"I wasn't exactly frank with you either, was I, letting you think I was a man."

His hand went to her shoulder and pulled her

closer, nestling her head in the crock of his neck. "You were always mean to me," he teased softly in her ear. "I think you turned Tom against me as well. He all but cut me dead when I tried to help him."

"Yes, because I warned him away from you. A pity he hadn't remembered I also warned him away from the duke."

His head came up. "Was Crymont the cause of his debts?"

"Crymont, a Mrs. Reno, his own stupidity, and of course his inexperience. But he is coming along nicely. He says he will redeem my diamonds."

Havergal remembered the necklace and rifled in his pocket for the box. "I got them yesterday. My final grand gesture." He handed her the box.

"One more gesture than my selfish nature would have made, under the circumstances," she said with a flush of pride for his generosity. "Thank you, Jacob. Tom will pay you for them." She looked out the window at meadows and a farm and said, "Your groom is going the wrong way! We seem to be heading into the country."

"I told Crooks to take a spin out the Chelsea Road before driving to the hotel."

She turned a suspicious eye on him. "Why?"

"Because there aren't so many carriages here. Since I am now a respectable working lord, I must set a good example. It wouldn't do for me to be making love in a crowded city. I can just imagine the cartoons!"

His arms closed around her, and in view of a passing curricle and a mounted rider, his reformed lips found hers for a ruthless kiss. Her head spun, and the blood in her veins felt like brandy. It was another unreal moment. Jacob loved her. In spite of the unlikelihood—her modest means and background, her greater age, and her astringent nature—he loved her. She returned the pressure of that embrace, swelling with joy and opening herself to the pleasure of love. When she opened her eyes, she saw the mounted rider peering through the window with the liveliest curiosity.

She pulled away, embarrassed. Havergal saw where she was looking and waved to the rider. "That was Sir Alfred Moreland, an honorable member of the opposition. You'll have to marry me, to save my reputation," he said. She smiled softly, and he added, "That wasn't a very elegant proposal, was it, darling? I'll do better, when we have more privacy."

"I'm sure you will."

"And perhaps—just a suggestion—you might work up enough interest to supply an answer?"

"I wouldn't want to contribute to your poor reputation."

"That wasn't a very elegant acceptance either."

"I have very little experience in saying yes. I'll do better, too, when we have more privacy. I know you don't care what others might say about your marrying an older lady, Jacob, but—" He gave a *tsk* of dismissal. "What—what do you think your father will have to say about this engagement?"

"He will say 'Amen' and breathe a sigh of relief. I have already discussed you with Papa. He hoped for something of the sort when he encouraged me to dash off to Norton's place. He had already met you and urged you not to give up Horace's trust. I would have proposed before I left Ashford if I had realized Papa approved. I fully intended to marry you, with or without his approval, but preferably with. I have not been a good son. I hope to be a better one in future."

"Your father didn't suggest anything of the sort to *me*," she replied doubtfully.

"Nor to me, till I told him my feelings. He knew

that would be the likeliest way to get my back up. But then I don't have to tell you about the obstinacy of my nature, Lettie. It was when you gave me that Bear Garden jaw that I began to appreciate you. I couldn't imagine any lady not falling for my drunken charm and debauchery."

"It is always a challenge for a lady to reform a hardened rake," she said blandly.

He gave her a challenging smile. "I must bear that in mind and not become too tame a husband."

"And I must keep my claws sharp, to keep you in line."

"A round of the bubbly!" Norton decreed when he heard the announcement of their betrothal. "Glad to hear you two are joining the society of us old married folks. Yessir, there is nothing like a good woman, eh laddie? Unless it is a good man, heh, heh."

"Or even a bad one," Havergal added. Norton shot him a sharp look. "I mean myself, Ned. *You* are the salt of the earth."

"So are you, laddie. I would have to say Lettie has done pretty well for herself—a title and a fortune—at her age! And you are not at all an ill-favored lad for looks either. I had no idea this match was brewing. I had the notion Lettie thought you were—Heh, heh, obviously I was mistaken."

Lettie and Havergal exchanged a private smile. "Yes, obviously we were mistaken," Lettie allowed. "And now let us make that toast."

216

Regency...

HISTORICAL ROMANCE
AT ITS FINEST